THE HOUSE ON CEMETERY HILL

A MYSTERY SEARCHERS BOOK

BARRY FORBES

THE HOUSE ON CEMETERY HILL

A MYSTERY SEARCHERS BOOK

VOLUME 4

By
BARRY FORBES

BAKKEN
BOOKS

ISBN 978-1-955657-21-1
For Worldwide Distribution
Printed in the U.S.A.

Published by Bakken Books
2022

AMAZING BOOK! My daughter is in 6th grade and she is home-schooled, she really enjoyed reading this book. Highly recommend to middle schoolers. *Rubi Pizarro on Amazon*

I have three boys 11-15 and finding a book they all like is sometimes a challenge. This series is great! My 15-year-old said, "I actually like it better than Hardy Boys because it tells me currents laws about technology that I didn't know." My reluctant 13-year-old picked it up without any prodding and that's not an easy feat. *Shantelshomeschool on Instagram*

I stumbled across the author and his series on Instagram and had to order the first book! Fun characters, good storyline too, easy reading. Best for ages 11 and up. *AZmommy2011 on Amazon*

Virtues of kindness, leadership, compassion, responsibility, loyalty, courage, diligence, perseverance, loyalty and service are characterized throughout the book. *Lynn G. on Amazon*

Barry, he LOVED it! My son is almost 14 and enjoys reading but most books are historical fiction or non-fiction. He carried your book everywhere, reading in any spare moments. He can't wait for book 2 – I'm ordering today and book 3 for his birthday. *Ourlifeathome on Instagram*

Perfect series for our 7th grader! I'm thrilled to have come across this perfect series for my 13-year old son this summer. We purchased the entire set! They are easy, but captivating reads and he is enjoying them very much. *Amylcarney on Amazon*

DISCLAIMER

Prescott, the former capital of the Arizona Territory, is considered by many to be the state's crown jewel. Aside from this central Arizona locale, *The Mystery Searchers* series is a work of fiction. Names, characters, businesses, places, events, incidents, and other locales are either the products of the author's imagination or used in a fictitious manner. Any resemblance to actual persons, living or dead, or actual events is purely coincidental.

Read more at www.MysterySearchers.com

For Linda,
whose steadfast love and encouragement
made this series possible

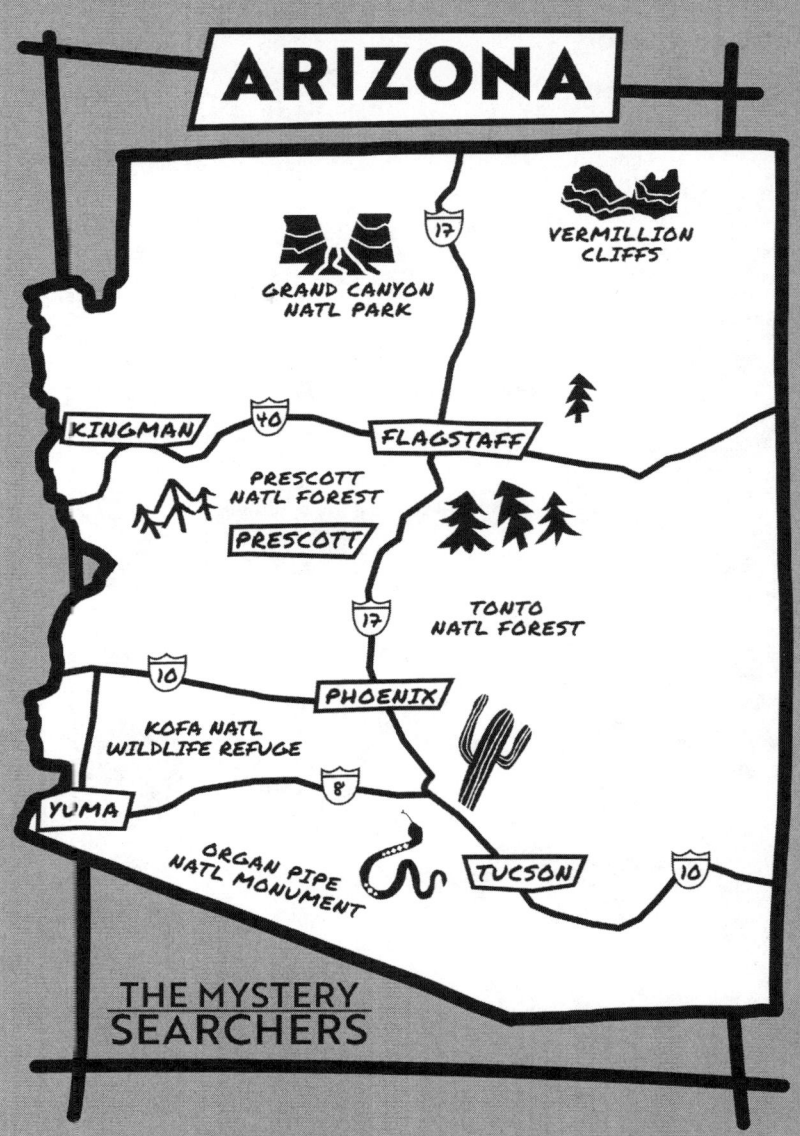

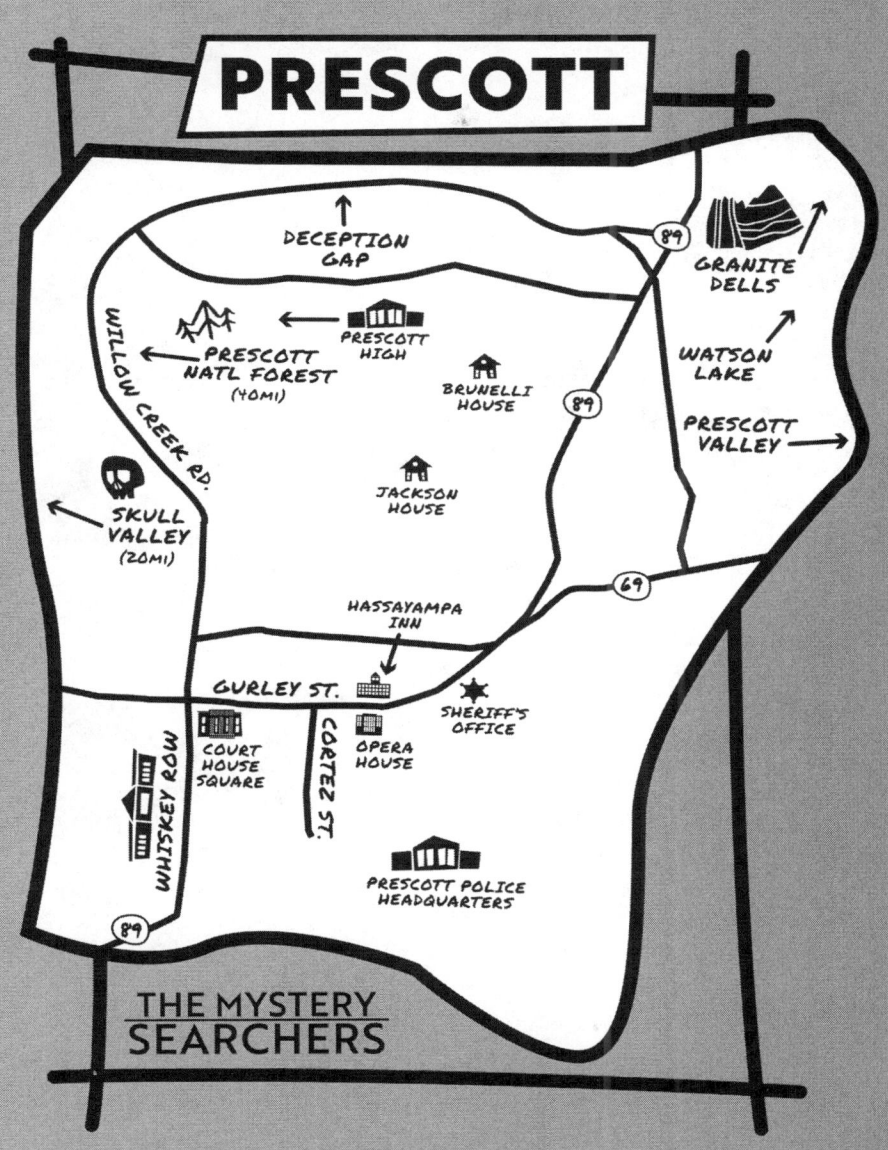

A STRANGER ARRIVES

"He *died*? He's dead? Whatever do you mean, Mrs. McPherson?"

Suzanne stared at the woman, dumbfounded. To judge from her hands, she had to be in her seventies. But you'd never have known it from looking at her face—or her style. She wore jeans, sneakers, and a sleeveless top. Her alert, bright eyes darted around the room. Short bleached-blond hair and a facelift—or two?—gave her a younger appearance, but her perfume was *way* too strong.

Suzanne shot a glance at her brother. Nothing the older woman had said made any sense. *Not even close.*

The drama had begun at nine fifteen that morning, right after the twins' parents left for the grocery store. While Tom struggled to get out of bed, Suzanne was brushing her long, auburn hair into a ponytail. The doorbell rang. She bolted downstairs and opened the front door, expecting to see Pete and Kathy. *They're very early*, it occurred to her.

Instead, a tiny older lady stood outside, her nose pressed against the screen. Suzanne, tall and willowy like her brother, looked down in surprise.

"Well, hello," she said, greeting the visitor with her customary warmth.

"Are you Suzanne Jackson?"

"Why, yes, I sure am. How may I help you?"

With an unexpected tug, the screen door opened and the woman —all five feet of her—brushed past Suzanne and marched straight into the house.

"Hey, wh-what are you doing?" a stunned Suzanne called after her.

The lady ignored her. "Is your father home?"

"No, he sure isn't."

"Good. Where's your computer?" It wasn't a question; it was a demand.

"Tom!" Suzanne cried out. Whenever someone thought of her, *confident* was the word that came to mind. She knew where she was going in life and wasn't easily rattled. But now, at this moment, her confidence had vanished. She couldn't figure out if she felt angry, scared, or both. But who could fear a five-foot-tall old lady?

Alarmed at his sister's tone, Tom raced downstairs as he threw on his bathrobe. "What's the matter, Suzie?"

"This woman just walked right into our house!" Suzanne hissed. "Like she owns it."

The older lady stood in the living room, her arms folded, refusing eye contact, appearing all but oblivious to the consternation around her.

Tom moved closer, forcing the stranger to focus on him. "What can we do for you?"

"Are you Tom Jackson?" She had an authoritative manner—like a person accustomed to issuing orders and always getting her own way.

"Yes, I am," he replied rather stiffly.

"Good," she said with a satisfied expression. "I need you both. Where's your computer?"

"It's right *there*," Suzanne said, her exasperation pouring into the open. Her face flushed as anger welled up inside her. She gestured to the corner desk in the living room, jabbing with an index finger. "Who *are* you, and what do you want with our computer?"

"I am Mrs. Leslie McPherson," the lady replied, drawing herself up as tall as she could with obvious pride. "And I don't *want* your stupid computer. I want to *show* you something."

"Okay," Tom said, but it wasn't. Quiet, thoughtful, and solid —"Like the Rock of Gibraltar, you can always count on him!" as one of his baseball coaches liked to say—Tom felt upended. He couldn't figure the woman out. She was, well, *odd*. Maybe worse. "There it is. Go for it."

"*You* go for it," she commanded. "Plug this thing in." An old-fashioned thumb drive appeared in her open hand.

That's when Tom's curiosity kicked into high gear. Technology of any kind, no matter how minor, intrigued him—he was a founding member of Prescott High's award-winning technology club. Tom plucked the drive from Mrs. McPherson's outstretched palm with two fingertips, trying his best not to touch her, all the while keeping a sharp eye on the woman. *No telling what she'll do next,* he thought, *but this is interesting.* He sat down at the desk and inserted the device in one of the laptop's USB ports.

Suzanne took a deep breath and calmed herself. Polite but guarded, she pulled over a loveseat behind her brother. "Please sit down," she said. Mrs. McPherson perched on the edge of the cushion, looking over Tom's shoulder. Suzanne joined her, keeping a safe distance between herself and their peculiar guest.

"There's only one file on it," Tom said, noting its format. "Video footage, I guess."

"Brilliant," the woman replied sharply. "Go to eleven twenty-eight."

The monitor lit up, displaying a grainy night scene: a wide-angle view of a parking lot and, across a two-lane roadway, an outdated-looking single-story office building with a few vehicle spaces in front. A dull light shone out through the glass lobby doors. High above the building's entryway appeared a company name, McPherson Construction. The LED signage blazed in the darkness, casting a sickly green glow over the entire façade. The parking spots outlined on the asphalt, tight up against the structure, all sat empty.

Tom fast-forwarded a little, until the day/time stamp in the lower right corner of the screen read FRIDAY JUNE 8 11:28:00 PM. Seconds clicked by on the digital clock.

"Just last night?" Suzanne asked.

"Mmm-hmm," Mrs. McPherson replied.

"Is that your company?" Tom wondered aloud.

"What do you think?"

"There's no cause for rudeness," Suzanne said, ticked off again and letting it show. Mrs. McPherson, staring straight ahead, sniffed and ignored the admonition.

"What are we waiting for?" Tom asked.

On the screen, a car swooshed by in a blur along the two-lane street. Obviously, someone had installed a camera on the far side of the roadway.

"Patience," she replied.

Unseen by her, Tom rolled his eyes. Suzanne suppressed a wry smile.

A late-model Nissan sedan slowed and turned in. The driver skipped the parking places, pulling into deep shadows to the right of the building. If someone drove past, Tom noted—beat cops in a patrol car, for example—the vehicle would be all but invisible.

In the grainy footage, they watched the brake lights fade. A smallish man stepped into the night and hurried to the front door. It took a few seconds—he had a key—before the door swung open. He walked in, closing it after him, and disappearing down a dimly lit corridor.

It wasn't possible to see the man's face. Not once did he look back, and anyway the footage was far too grainy. The luminous signage threw off a steady glow, but visibility was marginal. The vehicle's rear license plate, sheltered from light, was unreadable.

"Who is he?" Suzanne asked.

"Philip Edward Marsden, and he's a con man and a thief."

Tom turned and locked eyes with her. "What did he do?"

"He robbed McPherson Construction—twice. The first time he stole a corporate entity we owned called Old Blue Dog Company. Then he hit us again—last night—which is what we're watching here. He helped himself to fifty-two hundred bucks and an antiquated computer."

"No way!" the twins chorused.

"Yup. The little maggot's building a nest somewhere," Mrs. McPherson said with certainty. She had a sarcastic manner of speaking, and a habit of talking with her hands, her arms flailing in the air.

"That's a lot of money," Suzanne said.

"You bet your life it is. He swiped it right out of my office safe, leaving it wide open. There's no doubt in my mind that he must have stolen the combination months ago. And Zeke lent him that computer—looks as if he wanted it back."

"So Marsden used to work for you?" Suzanne said. "And who's Zeke?"

Mrs. McPherson ignored the questions. She paused, seeming to gather her thoughts. "That's when it hit me: Philip Marsden has returned." She spoke tensely as her hands continued to bob and weave in the air. Suzanne slid further away on the loveseat to avoid getting whacked; the eccentric lady didn't even notice. "No rational soul would want that piece of computing junk—it's older than dirt."

"So he has a key to the building..." Suzanne said, wondering why.

"No kidding," Mrs. McPherson replied. "Turns out he made a copy before—now jump to eleven thirty-seven."

Tom scanned forward and hit *Play*. They watched as the same man stepped out the front door—a mid-size cardboard box tucked under one arm—and locked it behind him. He turned to look both ways before slipping back to his car. Even then, the dark, grainy footage barred any possibility of identifying him. His face was nothing but a soft blur. Moments later, his vehicle backed out and zoomed away—still without affording clear visibility of its license plates.

Ye- Mrs. McPherson plainly had no doubts as to the man's identity. "So last night, he came, he saw, he conquered," she quipped, deadpan. "Which, when you think about it, is bat-crazy weird."

"Why is that?" Tom asked, half afraid of what she'd say next.

"Because Philip Marsden died five weeks ago."

2

BACK FROM THE DEAD?

That's when Suzanne responded in shock. *"He died?* He's dead? Whatever do you mean, Mrs. McPherson?"

"What do you *think* I mean?" the older lady replied, glaring at Suzanne and pursing her lips. "A stiff is a stiff." She paused. *"The Daily Pilot* said so too. Philip Marsden appeared on the obituary page a month ago."

She reached into her purse, a cavernous black affair that rested at her feet. A few seconds passed before she retracted a folded sheet of paper, neatly cut from a newspaper.

"Here," she said, thrusting it into Tom's hands. "Read it yourself."

Tom unfolded the clipping and smoothed it out on the desk. Suzanne craned her neck to see. Sure enough, Philip Marsden's name appeared at the top of the obituary, together with his birth and death dates. "A graduate of the University of Arizona's College of Business," it read. Died on the seventh of May from a rare degenerative autoimmune disease. No survivors. And no picture, either.

Dead at twenty-six, one month earlier.

According to Mrs. McPherson, it was the same guy who they had just watched in the video.

"I—I don't get it," Suzanne stammered. "If he died a month ago, what's he doing on the security footage from last night?"

"Good question," the older lady replied. "That's why you're here."

"We *live* here," Tom retorted, his annoyance, like his sister's, finally spilling over. "Why are *you* here?"

"Are you kidding?" she responded. Her thin eyebrows edged up, one higher than the other, as her voice rose in volume by a decibel or two. "Aren't you the mystery searchers I read about in *The Daily Pilot*? More than once too. You solve mysteries, and this is a weird one."

She stopped and looked away. "Philip Marsden is dead or alive— there's nothing in between. And it's my contention that he's alive and well." Then her eyes ticked back to the twins as she tossed out an obvious challenge: "Get it?"

Silence. Tom turned and stared hard at Mrs. McPherson. He couldn't figure her out. Was her demeanor little more than a charade, or was this her real self? Or was she just flat-out crazy? One thing he knew for sure: a highly volatile lady was sitting behind him. *Maybe even dangerous*, he thought.

"Okay," Tom said, trying his best to maintain calm. His patience had run low. Worse, he didn't like the woman. Not at all. "You've lost us. Please provide background here—we need to understand what's happening."

"Pay attention," Mrs. McPherson ordered. "I'm only going through this once." It seemed people didn't argue with her. Not ever.

"McPherson Construction is the largest building group in Prescott," she explained. "My husband, Zeke, died last March, leaving the business in my capable hands—more capable than his, anyway. Before he passed on, Zeke allowed Philip Marsden the use of one of our offices. My husband was a patsy for sob stories. He brought home stray cats, lost dogs, and human losers. He found this one—or the maggot found *him*—at a country club luncheon. Marsden sat right beside Zeke. The little weasel was enjoying free food, I'm sure, and eating his way into Zeke's soft heart. He told my husband he had experienced a terrible, unfair bankruptcy and needed office space to start over again. That was a lie." She sniffed again. "The first of many."

Someone knocked on the front door.

"That'll be our friends, Kathy and Pete," Suzanne said, bolting over to greet them, wondering how to tell the Brunelli siblings that Mrs. McPherson had upended the first Saturday of their summer vacation. Their plans—including a doubles tennis match to celebrate—had just evaporated.

The Brunellis—shorter than the tall, willowy twins, but always striking with their coal-black hair and olive-hued skin—trailed in, surprised to see an unfamiliar lady in the living room. Introductions followed. Suzanne pulled out two folding chairs.

All the while, Mrs. McPherson sat immobile, looking ahead—her chilly, aloof self. She barely acknowledged the Brunellis until Tom mentioned that they were the other half of their team—the four mystery searchers, as *The Daily Pilot*, Prescott's hometown newspaper, had called them.

"Oh, sure," Mrs. McPherson said, turning to study the newcomers for the first time. She winked at them. "You're in for a treat. Ever see a dead man walking?"

The twins backed up to retell the story. Tom ran the video again. The older lady made an impatient sound before interrupting.

"Zeke offered Marsden an unused office with a big old desk. 'So he can start over, till he gets back on his feet,' he told me. I objected, but it did no good, of course. Once Zeke made up his mind…" One hand gestured about, showing her dissatisfaction.

"In one of its drawers, we had stored our files on a newish corporate entity—Old Blue Dog Company, named after Zeke's favorite hunting dog. We registered it two years ago. Plus we printed letterheads and envelopes and ordered a corporate seal and all that." She paused to catch her breath. "But we never rolled it out. Stupid idea and far too expensive. Why Zeke ever thought he needed to create a company just to offer a new building technique for connecting rafters, I'll never understand."

Mrs. McPherson pursed her lips again. "To be honest, I had forgotten all about it. But that didn't stop Philip Marsden. He stole Old Blue Dog Company—the incorporation papers, corporate seal, stationary, the entire file, everything."

"Why would he do that?" Pete asked. He was the impetuous one who always went straight to the point.

"Your guess is as good as mine, but I'll tell you one thing—whatever his intentions, you can bet they weren't honest. My secretary, Pat, discovered the theft quite by accident, when she was looking for a misplaced file. I questioned Marsden." Her eyes burned. "The little creep flew into a rage—I couldn't *believe* it. Right then, I demanded that he return his office key and threw him out. 'Don't come back,' I told him. *Ever.*"

Mrs. McPherson's sharp eyes scoured the faces around the room. "He ignored me, of course. At that stage, I didn't realize how dangerous the man could be. But I'd still have tossed the maggot out on his ear!"

The foursome believed her.

"Who said he was dangerous?" Suzanne asked.

"The police," she replied. "I called them to charge Marsden with theft and fraud—and anything else I could think of—after he swiped the Old Blue files. They ran a background check. Turns out, he had served time in the state prison in Florence. If someone crossed him behind bars, the cops told me, Marsden had a penchant for going crazy—I witnessed *that* with my own eyes. There were violent incidents in prison that added to his sentence. The parole board released him one week before he met my husband. One week! Can you *believe* it?" Her voice cracked. "I need water."

Kathy raced to the adjoining kitchen and returned with a full glass. Mrs. McPherson took a big gulp and set the glass on the floor beneath her.

"The man's a con artist, that's for sure. He talked and acted like a big-time corporate executive. Dressed like one too. Said he was Harvard-educated—another lie from a two-bit shyster. No wonder Zeke fell for his line." Mrs. McPherson's voice dropped lower with disgust. "A month later, we heard he had developed a fatal autoimmune disease. Something rare, with a long name. I don't remember —I don't care. Then his obituary appeared in the newspaper."

Kathy asked, "Who told you about his illness?"

"His landlady. She called me after Marsden moved to a hospice. I informed the police, but they had already abandoned their investigation. *Why?* Because they had ordered the little maggot down to the station for questioning. He denied stealing anything—never heard of Old Blue Dog Company, he said. So they obtained a search warrant and went through his room. Nothing. Without proof, the police dropped the case. I get it, but it was a stupid move. In fact, I told them so."

The twins glanced at each other with knowing eyes, hoping their parents had stopped for coffee and wouldn't return soon.

Suzanne said, "Then he showed up on the security footage."

"Yup. A stiff that's alive and well," Mrs. McPherson said with a grimace. "A rare occurrence, is it not? I'll tell you what, I had my suspicions. After I read the obituary notice, I called the police again. They checked things out and confirmed it—said the man had died." She muttered a bad word. "Now we know better, don't we?"

"Shouldn't you show this video to the police?" Pete asked.

Mrs. McPherson glared at him. "You're kidding, right? You know what they'd say? 'No way can you tell that's Philip Marsden. And anyway, he's dead.' Oh, sure, we can't see his face—I grant you that. But I'd recognize that slimy character in the dark." She chuckled for the first time. "In fact, I did. And he's a long way from dead. And besides, I've given up on the police. I'm counting on *you* now."

Then she muttered, under her breath, darkly, "But I might call them for insurance purposes."

"Why would he fake his own death?" Kathy asked. "I mean, it seems rather drastic."

"I'll tell you what's drastic," Mrs. McPherson said, her voice shooting higher. "If the authorities found him guilty of theft, or worse, they'd ship him right back to the slammer. It could be years before the little creep saw daylight again. When you're an ex-convict on parole, it's not a smart idea to get busted for anything—not even a speeding ticket. No matter what, he had to stop the police investigation."

"Dying will do that," Suzanne said. It was all beginning to make sense to her.

The older woman smiled. "Now you're getting it. Marsden knew a conviction would earn him a one-way ticket to Florence." She snorted. "Heck, he might even have earned his old cell back. It'd be a shame, wouldn't it?"

"Wasn't he aware of the security camera?" Kathy asked.

"Nope." She heaved a sigh and appeared to relax a little. "The camera belongs to the company across the street. It focuses on *their* parking lot, which is much bigger than ours—it stretches out in front of their building, and our headquarters is in the background. That's why it's fuzzy. We've never had our own security system—Zeke insisted we didn't need one, that it'd be a waste of time. He always was too trusting. Cheap too. First thing this morning, after I realized someone had raided the safe, I walked over and asked to check their footage. My hunch was right—*Marsden*. Then I came here."

"You mentioned that he stole fifty-two hundred dollars," Tom said. "Did he take *all* of the cash on-hand?"

"He sure did," she replied. "We keep it to pay day laborers—we could have a dozen of them working at the same time. That's common in construction—though not every company is as meticulous as we are in our cash accounting. One thing Zeke and I always agreed upon: everything by the book. Marsden cleaned it all out."

"Besides yourself, who else knows the combination to the safe?" Kathy asked.

"Only my secretary, Pat. And she's worked at the company even longer than I have."

Suzanne wondered aloud, "So how did Marsden get the combination?"

"The only thing we could think of," Mrs. McPherson replied, "was this." She tugged a worn, tiny scrap of paper from a side pocket of her purse and held it up: about two by three inches, with a series of numbers scrawled across it. "Zeke left this hidden under a pencil tray in one of his desk drawers. I had no idea. That weasel Marsden must have gone mooching around Zeke's office one night after work and found it. After Zeke died, we left his desk, his whole office, exactly the way it was. I can't—*we* can't bear to change a thing."

For the first time since she had walked in, Mrs. McPherson's hard façade had cracked—a little. Suzanne almost felt like hugging her but...

"Well," Tom said gently, "that would explain it."

Pete's face showed doubt. "Why would Marsden expose himself to such a risk? If they convicted him of a crime, he'd go back to jail —and for a long haul too. It's not *that* much money."

"Maybe not to you," Mrs. McPherson replied, her eyes boring into him with scorn. "But I haven't the faintest idea why he was willing to take the risks he took. What am I, my brother's keeper?"

At that moment the front door opened. The twins' mother, Sherri, walked in and headed for the kitchen without a glance. Behind her, carrying two bags of groceries, was Edward Jackson —*Chief* Edward Jackson of the Prescott City Police.

"These are our parents," Suzanne said proudly as she eyed the older woman. "Mom and Dad, this is Mrs. Leslie McPherson."

Mrs. McPherson had recognized their well-known father. She stood up, ramrod straight, unwittingly kicking over the glass of water at her feet and staring at the Chief with ice-cold steely eyes. "Well, why on earth doesn't your police force *do something!*"

Then she strode across the living room and out the front door, slamming it behind her with a deafening *bang!*

3

THE HUNT BEGINS

The Chief set the groceries on the kitchen countertop before turning toward the foursome. "So what's new with Leslie?"

Tom's astonishment rippled out. *"You know her?"*

"For thirty years," his father replied, stepping into the living room. "Plus, your grandfather dated her in high school."

"What?" Suzanne exclaimed. She paused in mopping up the pool of water Mrs. McPherson had spilled and looked up. *"Papa dated her? That would be… sixty years ago!"*

"Uh-huh. More. They attended Prescott High together," the Chief said. "She was a country girl. Rode a bus to school every day."

"I can't believe it!" Tom blurted. "That's one heck of a coincidence."

"You bet," Sherri said, stepping back into the living room. "She married Zeke McPherson, a friend of your grandfather's."

"Just think," Kathy quipped, her eyes dancing. "But for a quirk of fate, she'd show up in your family tree. She'd be your granny!"

The twins groaned as laughter burst out around the room.

"Don't be too hard on her," the Chief advised. "She's one tough businesswoman, smart too. Right now she's busy chasing a ghost named Philip Marsden. I assume that was the reason for her visit?"

"That's what she told us," Suzanne replied, nodding.

"Check out the security video she brought," Tom urged, turning back to the computer. "It's interesting." The older lady had stomped out before retrieving her thumb drive. The twins' parents gathered around.

"Well, there's the culprit," the chief said as Tom paused the video after the thief's exit. "No doubt. But we can't identify anyone from footage like that. And the license plate number is indistinct as I'm sure you've noticed already. How much did the guy steal?"

"Fifty-two hundred dollars."

"That's a goodly amount," the Chief said. "If she files a complaint, we'll open an investigation. But she needs to make the first move."

"Do you mind if we help her?" Suzanne asked her father.

Tom frowned. "Do we *want* to help her?"

Their mother spoke up. "Of course you do. The poor woman is desperate even if she didn't show it. Otherwise, she wouldn't have come."

"She's far from poor," the Chief argued. "Leslie owns the city's top construction group."

"You know what I mean," Sherri retorted.

"Why not?" Pete jumped in. "It's an interesting mystery, for sure. How often does a dead man walk?"

"Don't hold your breath," Kathy replied coolly, nudging her brother. "But let's do it. We'll soon figure out if Mr. Marsden is dead or alive."

The Chief's chortled. "Sure, go ahead. But trust me, it'll be a wild ride. Leslie is a tiger with a temper. You can never predict what she'll do next."

EARLY THAT SAME AFTERNOON, THE FOUR MYSTERY SEARCHERS JUMPED into the Mustang Hatchback. The famous muscle car—given to the Brunellis in gratitude for helping to solve the last case—had been abandoned in a mysterious mansion's garage, decades earlier. But today, much to Pete's displeasure, Kathy was at the wheel. Her driver's license had recently arrived in the mail. Now the siblings shared driving roles.

"I'm slower than he is," Kathy said, annoying her brother—which she loved to do. "Pete suffers from a heavy foot."

"If you opened your mouth any further, you'd fall in," he sniped.

"Apparently, it's you who suffers from my sense of humor," Kathy shot right back, tossing her head. Her long, black ponytail flipped around. The Mustang's throaty growl kicked in as the hatchback pulled away from the curb.

Bickering aside, the Brunelli siblings got along well. They looked enough alike that strangers assumed they were twins, but their natures were polar opposites. Kathy was a noisy, natural-born comic. Her quirky sense of humor was a gift from her mother, Maria, a registered nurse who worked part-time in the emergency-room at Prescott Regional Hospital. Pete, a year older, was the quiet but plucky to a fault, much like his father, Joe—an entrepreneur and the founder and editor of a popular national magazine that focused on world history.

First stop was police headquarters. Detective Joe Ryan—a good friend and an unassuming investigator who had assisted them on two previous cases—had agreed to a last-minute meeting. He greeted them in the entranceway wearing his trademark old suit and scuffed loafers. His western drawl always put people at ease.

"Great to see y'all." He thrust his hand out toward them.

Ryan was as short and bald as ever, of course, but they noticed that he was sporting a new pair of glasses with thinner lenses. Gone were the thick, Coke-bottle spectacles he had worn for years. The mystery searchers loved the man, and the Chief often claimed he was the best detective on the force.

Only one small conference room was available. The five of them squeezed into a tiny space built for four that stank of sweat and old smoke. *Ugh*, thought Suzanne. They soon brought Ryan up to speed

Pete said, "Then the Chief and Mrs. Jackson returned home."

"Mrs. McPherson yells out, 'Why doesn't your police force do something?'" Kathy said. She stifled a laugh. *Just the thought of it...*

"At which point the older lady stomped out and slammed the door," Suzanne explained. "It all happened so fast."

"I couldn't figure out if she was real or not," Tom said. "I mean, that lady is..."

"Crazy," Pete finished.

"Well, that's Leslie for sure," the investigator replied with a chuckle. "I've known her for years. She's quite unhappy with me—and with our whole department. The problem is, we're almost positive Philip Marsden is dead."

"Almost?" Pete asked.

The detective opened a folder that rested on the desk. "Without a body, nothing is guaranteed—they cremated him. Or someone else, I guess, if Leslie is right. But we're confident that he's dead." He leafed through the file. "Here's a head-and-shoulders shot of Mr. Marsden."

He passed around a four-by-six photograph. An attractive-looking man stared straight into the lens, the edges of his mouth lifting into a half smile. He had fair skin, piercing blue eyes, and blond hair brushed away from his forehead. A number appeared at the bottom of the photo, stamped next to the words FLORENCE STATE PRISON.

"Taken on his last day behind bars," Detective Ryan intoned, "before his release."

"Oh, wow," Suzanne said. She thought Marsden had a handsome face. "So this is a current shot?"

"Well, sort of," the investigator deadpanned. "He's dead. Remember?"

Suzanne reddened. "What do you know about him?"

"Born in Omaha," the investigator said. "His parents died in an auto accident when he was fourteen. He moved to Phoenix to live with his grandmother, but she passed away in his first year of college. Attended the University of Arizona and earned a degree in management. Proficient in computer programming—one of the brightest in his class, his professors told me. He has no known living relatives."

"Why was he in prison?" Pete asked.

"Fraud and grand larceny," Detective Ryan replied. "He scammed a large corporation headquartered in Tucson by hacking into its secure site. Transferred three million to an account in Singapore. Then he shipped it electronically to multiple countries—like a daisy chain—before it ended up in a Swiss bank account. His, as things turned out."

Tom whistled. "Three million! That's a lot of dough."

"Yeah," the detective said. "He was a high-tech genius, but it got him into a world of trouble. Not as smart as he thought. He spent three years in the pen."

Tom's mind raced. "Okay. Mrs. McPherson claims he 'stole' Old Blue Dog Company. And he's a high-tech guy, very sophisticated too—it's not just everyone who can hack into a secure site. What could he do with a corporation that had never rolled out?"

"There's no telling," Detective Ryan replied. "We checked the corporate records of Old Blue Dog Company. No change since the day they registered it. And no evidence of its use, either, online or off. Nothing. And," he added, raising one finger in the air, "Mr. Marsden denied any culpability. Without proof or at least *some* clue, we can't do a thing. I tried to explain that to Leslie, but she wasn't in any mood to listen."

The room went silent. There were no answers. Not yet.

"Well, here's the thumb drive," Suzanne said, handing it across the table. The investigator pulled up a laptop, careful not to bang his chair against the wall, and plugged in the drive. The group screened the security footage in silence, running the segments they had already viewed—twice.

"It could be anyone," Detective Ryan said. He pushed back from the conference room table as far as possible. "It's not Marsden. Maybe Leslie has a problem with one of her employees she doesn't know about—or doesn't want to face. Dead people don't commit crimes. Philip Marsden is in that category."

"What drove you to that conclusion?" Tom asked, sounding very businesslike.

"DeMaso's Funeral Home confirmed it. They handled the arrangements and cremated his body—and no one else's. Mr. Marsden's remains are in a plot on Cemetery Hill."

"Which means Mrs. McPherson must be wrong," Kathy said.

The detective replied with a grimace. "*Dead* wrong."

"So he couldn't have robbed the construction company," Pete said.

"Correct."

"That news won't sit well with Mrs. McPherson," Suzanne pondered.

"What else is new?" Tom said, forcing smiles around the room.

4

WINNING THEM OVER

It was late in the afternoon when the Mustang nosed into a parking spot at the front entrance of McPherson Construction. A sign stated that the offices were closed on Saturday. Still, an old Caddy parked out front. *Someone* was there.

Pete tried the door. "It's unlocked." They trooped into the lobby. The receptionist's desk was vacant but a hunting dog—a handsome black Labrador Retriever—sat looking through a window, staring into the street with unseeing eyes.

"Taxidermy," Tom said. "Mr. McPherson must have had his dog stuffed after it died."

"What a beautiful animal!" Suzanne exclaimed, walking over to pat the top of its head. She loved dogs—so much that the taxidermy didn't creep her out.

Kathy felt differently. She took a deep breath. "*Yeesh!* So *that* is Old Blue."

"*Was*," Pete corrected her.

"Very astute of you."

The foursome headed down a central corridor that smelled like sawdust. They hadn't gone far when an abrasive voice called, "Who's there?"

THE HOUSE ON CEMETERY HILL

Tom frowned before muttering, "That would be her." The woman still annoyed him.

A light shone from one office. Suzanne stopped at the doorway. "Hello, Mrs. McPherson. May we come in?"

The older lady sat at her desk, glaring at the foursome over the top of her reading glasses. A pen rested in her hand, a monitor and keyboard angled toward her before neatly stacked piles of papers. Her office was large, more like a conference room, with a handful of empty chairs arrayed in a semi-circle.

In the far-right corner squatted an old black safe, about four feet high and three feet wide, its door shut tight.

"What do you want?" she growled.

"We want to help you," Kathy replied. They filed in without waiting for an invitation.

"How?"

Tom gingerly placed the thumb drive on her desk. "You came to our house for a reason. We're here to solve this mystery."

"Your father is the chief of police."

"That has nothing to do with anything," Suzanne retorted. "And you knew that when you rang our doorbell." *In fact, you barged in!* she almost said.

"Chief Jackson helps us, for sure. But we choose our own cases," said Kathy. "Or they choose us."

Mrs. McPherson stared at them hard, one by one, before she broke the silence with a deep sigh. "Okay, sit down. But please. Nobody calls me Mrs. McPherson. My name is Leslie."

Tom exhaled, realizing that he had been holding his breath. *She's unfreezing.* The four of them took seats in front of their new client.

"Philip Marsden is dead," Suzanne said, opening the discussion.

"He's as dead as I am!" the older woman exclaimed, throwing her head back and letting out a brassy laugh. Her eyes flashed around the room. "You've been talking to Detective Joe Ryan. Dead, my foot."

"Well, uh… Leslie," Tom said, "that's what someone at the funeral home told the police."

21

"Yeah, well, only one of us can be right," she replied, "and I'm betting on me." Her hands moved in tandem with her words, an index finger pointing toward herself.

Pete said, "That makes no sense. Why would they—?"

She cut him off. "That's for you to find out. Maybe they didn't lie, maybe they're just mistaken. It happens, you know."

"What makes you think Philip Marsden is alive?" Kathy asked.

That was the wrong question. "Did you not watch the security video?" Leslie demanded, her voice dripping sarcasm.

She never really asks, Tom reflected. *She orders.*

"Well… yeah," Kathy answered defensively. "You were with us."

"Okay. *That* is Mr. Marsden."

"But how do you *know*?" Suzanne asked, pushing harder. "The footage is so blurry."

"Easy. The man is on the short side. He's about five foot six, if that. And you can see that in the video when he stands at the front door. Next, follow him in—and out. He walks like a duck. How many people do you know who walk like a duck?" She paused.

Leslie snatched the thumb drive from her desk and inserted it into her computer. She pulled the keyboard closer and turned the monitor toward the foursome. Seconds later, the grainy footage appeared. They all stared at the screen as the man parked, stepped out of his car and hurried to the front door. Leslie froze the image.

"At his maximum height, the top of this head reaches right *here.*" Her finger touched the screen. "Now follow me."

She stood and walked down the central corridor. The four trailed behind her, filing past a startled Pat. Everyone stepped outside.

"Here you go," Leslie said, jabbing the doorframe. "The top of his head reached *here.*" She scanned their faces. "What does that make him?" she asked.

"My height," Kathy replied.

"About two inches shorter than I am," Suzanne stated, "and I'm five foot eight."

"Right on."

"Now you're giving me goose bumps," Kathy said.

Leslie said nothing and hustled back to her office.

Hard to believe she's in her seventies, Suzanne reflected.

"Now what else did you notice on the footage?" the older woman demanded. She sat back down at her desk.

For a moment, no one replied.

Pete broke the awkward silence. He couldn't hide that he was impressed. "The man walks like a duck."

Kathy said, "Well, that's awkward."

"See what I mean?" Leslie said triumphantly. Her arms shot straight up—like the goal posts on Prescott High's football field. "Welcome to *my* world!"

5

ELECTRONIC FOOTPRINTS

A subtle change had taken place, so gradual that no one noticed it at first.

Rather than issuing orders and delivering snarky remarks, Leslie was now engaging the four mystery searchers in perceptive conversation. Despite her sarcastic manner, she could be quite pleasant when she tried. Better yet, every so often her sharp tongue revealed a humorous edge.

"I ordered a security system," she informed them, "the first in McPherson Construction's history. And a locksmith is on the way. He'll change out the locks this afternoon. Just a little too late." She chortled. "If Zeke were still around, he'd go ballistic—kind of tight, if you know what I mean. Until now, the only problem we've ever had was a mailbox theft."

None of them could imagine anyone going ballistic on Leslie— even her husband. *Man, I'll bet she drove Zeke crazy*, Pete thought.

"Someone stole your mail?" Tom asked.

"Yeah. Two weeks ago Saturday. They smashed the locked letterbox by the front door. First time that's ever happened."

"Anyway, Marsden won't be making another appearance," Suzanne said to her.

She snorted. "He'd regret it, I can assure you."

No one doubted her.

Tom asked, "So what's he up to, Leslie? He stole Old Blue Dog Company for a reason, and he needs money. Somehow those two facts go together. Anything come to mind?"

She stopped for a few moments, lost in thought. "I wish. There's nothing that would give me more pleasure than to see Marsden behind bars."

"What about your conversations with him?" Kathy prompted.

Her brassy laugh rang out again. "Nada. I avoided him as much as possible. I couldn't stand the little weasel."

"Did he have friends?"

"I don't see how—he has the personality of a porcupine. No one ever came here asking for him. They wouldn't be welcome if they did."

"What did he do all day long?"

"Well... I'm told he surfed a lot on the Internet."

"How about calls?" Kathy asked. "Was he on his cell much?"

"It's funny you'd ask," Leslie said. Her thin eyebrows shot up once more, one higher than the other, making them look like sideways question marks. "In the last couple of weeks before his sudden departure, his cell phone buzzed more than ever before."

"Did Old Blue Dog Company have its own account at the bank?"

"What for? We never rolled it out."

"So no checks?"

"What do you think?" Leslie couldn't help herself.

"Did the company receive snail mail?" Tom asked.

"Just from the Arizona Corporation Commission," Leslie replied. "And the IRS. Bureaucratic junk mail. So annoying. We have to file an annual report and a nominal tax return once a year on Blue Dog's zero income and zero assets."

"Who does that?"

"Me, when I get around to it."

"Why not just shut Blue Dog down?" Tom wondered aloud.

"Why bother?" Leslie replied, "According to Detective Ryan,

there's no activity of any kind under that name. Besides, I can't quite bring myself to change anything my husband left behind."

The discussion wore on as the mystery searchers continued their hunt for clues. Leslie's personality changed like a chameleon, often too—switching from her combative, sarcastic mode into a pleasant persona and then back again.

Nothing else had bubbled to the surface. The meeting ended right after Tom said, "There's only one direction open to us. We either find Philip Marsden alive, or we prove that those ashes in the ground at Cemetery Hill are his."

"She's. . . close to likeable," Kathy said, as the two sibling pairs left her offices and stepped into the Mustang.

"Close doesn't count," Tom said.

"She's a leader," Suzanne said. The woman was growing on her.

"It had *something* to do with Zeke," Pete said.

Kathy giggled. "She doesn't think so."

———

On Sunday morning the two families attended St. Francis Church together, then met for their customary afternoon brunch. The four young detectives gathered at the end of the table, quietly hatching plans over delicious plates of Mexican food—cheese enchiladas, bean tostadas, and chimichangas, covered in the blistering-hot salsa they all loved.

"The hotter, the better," Pete said. Beads of sweat had popped out on his forehead.

"Arizona's food at its finest," Suzanne said between bites. "More hot sauce, please."

That evening, the foursome met in the Brunellis' family room. Each of them found a comfy spot in front of a computer screen—the twins had arrived with two laptops, Pete had plugged in his, and Kathy booted up the family room computer.

"Let's split this up," Tom advised. He was the technology guy. "If

Marsden is using the name Old Blue Dog Company online, we'll find electronic footprints *somewhere*."

"Detective Ryan's guys already did this," Kathy said, reminding them for the second time. She still sounded doubtful.

"Yeah," Tom replied, "but that was weeks ago. Could be nothing's changed, but you never know. Pete and I will start with the Arizona Corporation Commission."

"I'm in now," Pete said.

"Okay," Suzanne said, "I'll Google the name. Plus I'll try Bing, Yahoo, and AOL. Maybe Marsden is hiding out in the legacy Web, working through older engines like AOL and Yahoo. Each search engine uses a different database and search algorithm. We could get varied results."

Kathy hoped Tom's hunch was right. "I'll look for Philip Edward Marsden, starting with the social media platforms—Facebook, Twitter, LinkedIn, Instagram, and the rest."

"And check the Tucson newspaper archives while you're at it," Tom suggested. "The guy has a record, and I'm sure the press covered his trial."

For the next fifteen minutes, the only sound heard was the insistent tapping of fingers on keyboards. The Brunellis' parents, Joe and Maria, came and went twice, curious to see what was happening. Their mother brought glasses of icy-cold lemonade with an Italian twist: sprigs of fresh basil.

Kathy got the first hit. "You were right, Tom. Marsden's arrest and sentencing both appeared in the *Tucson Daily News* three years ago. Here's something interesting." She paused, trying to take it all in. "Police charged a guy named Robert Harman Maxwell as an accessory to Marsden's fraud scheme, but there wasn't enough evidence to convict him. They dropped the charges. I'll check him out."

There was a buzz around the room. "Where does he fit into the picture?" Suzanne asked. The soft sound of keyboard clicking started once more.

"Hey, wait a minute," Tom said later. "The McPhersons registered Old Blue Dog Company three years ago, but someone just notified the corporation commission of a change of address. The new address is a PO Box in Prescott's main post office!"

"When?" Pete asked.

"Three weeks ago."

"Oh, wow," Suzanne said.

"No wonder Detective Ryan's guys came up empty. They were *way* too early."

"Whoo-hoo!" Kathy cried out. "That means the company is active."

"There's more," Tom said, clicking away. "A week later, they officially deleted the name of a corporate officer—Zeke McPherson—and added a new guy. Guess who?"

"Philip Edward Marsden!" the others chorused.

"Nope: *Robert Harman Maxwell.*"

"I'm searching for him," Kathy said.

More time passed before Pete jumped up. "I got a hit too. Old Blue Dog Company filed a dba notice with the corporation commission. Old Blue is now doing business as 'A Better Retirement, Inc.'"

Kathy asked, "What's a dba?"

"Doing business as."

"When?" Tom asked.

"Ten days ago."

Tom looked up to the ceiling, thinking out loud. "*Hmmm.* So the public won't see the name Old Blue Dog Company—instead, the new face of the group is A Better Retirement. Clever. What on earth is *that* all about?"

"Well, they're going after older folks," Suzanne mused, "that's for sure. A lot of scammers do, you know." She turned back to her keyboard and started a new search.

Over the next thirty minutes, the domain name A Better Retirement appeared just once: on a domain registration site.

"Registered two weeks ago," Suzanne said. "But it's not live yet. They haven't rolled it out. It says *Reserved.*"

"They will."

"Only a matter of time."

Tom had quit tapping and sat very still, deep in thought.

Suzanne noticed. "What?"

"Well, Marsden notified the corporation commission of a change of address, right?"

"Sure, three weeks ago. We get that," his sister replied, sitting up and looking at him.

"My guess is the commission would have responded—in writing too, confirming the change of address. Leslie said she was the contact person and would automatically have received a notice of one kind or another. After that, any other notification—like a dba, for example, or a change of corporate officers—would go to the post office box, the new official address."

Kathy said, "There's something not right about this."

"Oh, sure," Pete said. "Devious. Smart too. Marsden figured he knew Leslie well. He was playing her."

"'Bureaucratic junk mail,' she called it, remember?" Suzanne said. "Maybe she let it pile up."

"Nope, she's too sharp for that," Tom said pointedly. "If she received a notice from the commission unexpectedly—not the normal time of year for reporting reminders—she would open it. Or Pat would. More likely she *never got it*. Remember that mailbox theft?"

"Whoa, wait a sec," Suzanne said. "*I forgot.* So Marsden made double sure to keep her out of that loop."

Tom said, "Yup, he did his homework. He found out that when the corporation commission received a notification, a letter would go out the next business day. So he notified them on a Thursday— that's what it says online—and the verification arrived in Leslie's mail on Saturday. Both dates check—they fit the change of address, *and* the theft."

Pete exclaimed, "I get it! And that same Saturday, Marsden ripped off Leslie's mail."

"Or one of his henchmen did," Suzanne said.

"So the other notifications never reached her. The horrible man was free to do his worst," Kathy said.

Meanwhile, a profile of Robert Harman Maxwell had showed up online. On LinkedIn, no less. "Got him," Kathy said.

"Who is he?" Suzanne asked.

"A classmate of Marsden's. They both graduated from the University of Arizona's College of Business the same year. And wait, look! Here's his picture." The other three gathered in front of Kathy's screen. Mr. Maxwell's U of A photo displayed a dour, pock-marked face with a deep frown, disjointed eyes, and greasy-looking long hair.

"I wouldn't want to run into him in the dark," Suzanne said.

Kathy shuddered instinctively.

6

THE STAKEOUT

On Monday night, a raging summer thunderstorm hovered over Prescott, dumping torrents of rain on the city streets. Lighting strikes lit up the skyline as the twins enjoyed the show from the front seat of their Chevy. They had parked in the lot reserved for Prescott's downtown post office together with three other cars which, they surmised, belonged to postal workers. Suzanne sat behind the wheel, munching on an apple.

It was half-past nine. On the radio, the Arizona Diamondbacks were hosting the LA Dodgers, an exciting game tied in the seventh inning. The loud volume swamped the hammering rain.

"The Diamondbacks will take it," Tom said.

"Too close to call."

Suzanne flipped the windshield wipers on and off. "Good thing they enclosed that stadium."

They sat facing the post office with a straight-shot view through a large window, just fifty yards away. Behind the glass were visible long rows of rental PO Boxes. The only one that concerned them was second from the top, fourth from the left: Box D21323.

According to the Arizona Corporation Commission, that box

represented the official mailing address of Old Blue Dog Company, now doing business as A Better Retirement, Inc.

The twins waited as time dragged past. They talked, argued, and laughed, all the while listening to the game and watching the light show in the sky. A Diamondback home run with two on base drew cheers.

Meanwhile, the rain slowed to a persistent drizzle.

The post office lock box section was accessible around the clock. The four mystery searchers had agreed to work in pairs to surveil it, taking three-hour shifts, hoping that Marsden, if he was alive, or one of his collaborators would pick up the mail. At nine o'clock the twins' shift had started. They had replaced the Brunellis, who in turn would replace them at midnight. Tom and Suzanne would return at three in the morning.

"Brutal," Kathy had complained earlier that same day as they were devising the plan.

"Yeah, but necessary," Suzanne said. "It's our only lead to find these guys. What choice do we have?"

"None. And in the start-up stage, chances are they'll be checking their mail often," Tom said.

"Besides, it's good for you," Pete said, looking at his sister and trying his best to annoy her. "You don't need your beauty sleep."

"Shut up."

"I only meant you're beautiful enough as it is."

"Right."

Every so often, one of the twins picked up a set of binoculars and trained their eyes on the post office. They had brought two pairs.

"Here comes another car," Tom said—the fourth one since their arrival. They ducked low as a late-model Nissan sedan pulled into the well-lit lot and parked close to the building. One driver, no passengers.

Peering just above the dashboard, they focused both sets of binoculars on the man. He swung his legs out of the car, his face angled away from them. Heavyset and on the short side, he wore a jacket and jeans. His feet touched the pavement. He stood and stretched which made his jacket pull above his waistline.

"He's armed, Suzie," Tom said tensely.

"Got it."

The jacket had slid over a holster before the man yanked it down. Then he stepped up to the front door, casual and relaxed, seemingly in no hurry, and into the post office, hanging a left.

"He's heading the right way," Suzanne said. She fired up the Chevy, peering through the binoculars and cranking the wipers on and off to clear the windshield. "Wait a sec, he's stopping in front of the boxes..." Her voice rose a little, though she didn't allow herself to feel too excited just yet.

She watched as the man pulled a key out of his box and reached up. *"It's a go, Tom!"*

She threw the Chevy into drive, shot across the lot, and parked two spaces from the Nissan. Tom slipped out the passenger door before the car had even stopped and hurried toward the post office entrance—arriving just in time. From inside, the man pushed the door open as he exited the building. He held the door open for Tom, who smiled at the guy and *casually* walked in. "Thanks."

"Sure."

Suzanne grabbed two quick photos with her cell phone—one of the Nissan's license plate, and a second of the man emerging from the post office as he glanced at Tom.

Inside, Tom hid around the corner for a few seconds—there was a six-foot span of wall between the door and the window—and retrieved an envelope from his back pocket. Then he stepped outside, holding his "mail" in one hand, and slid into the front seat of the Chevy.

The man sat in his Nissan, looking down. He hadn't moved an inch.

Tom muttered, "He's checking his mail."

"Let's skedaddle," Suzanne whispered.

"Why whisper?" Tom said. "He can't hear you."

She pulled away from the curb, past the Nissan—the guy glanced over as they cruised by—and drove out of the parking lot. Then she turned left and zoomed away.

"Suzie, can you say Robert Harman Maxwell?"

"No doubt about it. You can't miss that face. Long hair too."

Suzanne pulled over and parked as Tom called the Brunellis.

"It's him. He showed up."

"Him who?" Kathy asked.

"Robert Maxwell! And he's armed."

For seconds there was nothing but dead air. "We're on our way."

The twins felt at risk following the man—no way could he avoid noticing the Chevy. It was time for the Brunelli siblings and their hot Mustang to take over.

The drizzle continued. Maxwell's Nissan sedan headed northeast before turning onto Willow Creek Road. The Brunellis—who lived in the northern part of the city and were minutes ahead—pulled onto the same thoroughfare and parked at the side of the road. Pete turned off the ignition, the car went dark. He sat back, focused on his rearview mirror.

"He's gotta be almost here," Kathy said quietly, staring through a rain-soaked rear window. Then, a minute later, she cried out, *"There he is!"* Seconds later the Nissan whipped past, splattering their vehicle with pooled rainwater.

Pete started the Mustang—it had one of those old-fashioned keys—and waited a few moments before pulling into the right lane. Soon, he was speeding across Prescott's pitch-dark streets through puddles of water, maintaining a city block's distance from the Nissan. The Mustang's wipers flapped back and forth on their slowest setting.

Kathy texted progress messages. *We're close too*, Tom texted back.

Pete kept his distance, tracking the tail lights ahead. Kathy's bleary eyes seldom left her screen.

"Uh-oh, red light ahead," Pete said, slowing down. A pickup turned onto Willow Creek Road and pulled up behind the Nissan.

"Be careful not to alert him that we're tailing," Kathy advised.

"Well, at some point we'll catch up to him."

"That's okay—it'll look normal. The guy doesn't know us from a hole in the ground."

Pete changed lanes and stopped a few feet short beside Maxwell. The siblings checked out the vehicle from the corners of their eyes. The man's left hand and long, stringy hair shielded his face. There was nothing to see.

The light turned green. The Mustang growled off, but the Nissan hung back.

"He's just being careful," Pete said. "I think."

Kathy called Tom. "We had to pass him," she said without explaining why. "We're a block ahead, and he's falling back."

"Okay," Tom said. "So now he's between us. We're close—there are only two vehicles in front, and one of them is Maxwell's."

"Yup, the other guy is driving a pickup. Maxwell is leading in the right lane. How close are you?" Kathy asked.

"A block at most," Tom replied.

There wasn't far to go. The Nissan's brake lights glowed up as the vehicle slowed before making a hard right between a pair of high wrought-iron gates. Spike-topped vertical bars pointed ominously to a name spelled out in a stylized font, also in black iron, above. Someone had propped the gates open on both sides of a narrow roadway.

"*Whoa!*" Suzanne declared. She whisked a stray lock of auburn hair away from her eyes, straining to read through the streaked windshield. "You know what that is, right? No way are we going in there. He'd pick up on us in a heartbeat." She cruised past the turnoff, searching for somewhere to turn around.

"Guess he's stopping in to say hello to Marsden," Tom quipped.

Suzanne rolled her eyes. "In the middle of the night?"

The thief had vanished into the bleak and brooding precincts of Cemetery Hill.

7

CEMETERY HILL

Tuesday morning, only a few hours after the foursome's late-night adventure ended, the Chief left the house long before Tom and Suzanne had struggled out of bed.

"His emergency cell phone buzzed before sunup," Sherri explained to her disappointed twins at breakfast. They wanted to update their father and seek his advice.

"Well, you can always tell me," their mother said with a smile. The three of them talked for close to an hour. Sherri, a professional social worker, was a good listener.

Tom messaged the two pics over to Detective Ryan, together with an overview of the night's events.

A few minutes later, the investigator called. "That's Maxwell, all right. He registered that car in Tucson. I'll ask the patrol officers to keep an eye open for him."

Next, they cruised over to McPherson Construction, just a few blocks away. For the first time, they met Pat, the company's secretary and receptionist. A heavyset woman with glasses and white hair who looked to be around Leslie's age, she offered a firm, freckled handshake without moving from behind her desk.

"Welcome," Pat said with a warm smile. "Leslie told me all about you." They chatted for a minute. "I'm ancient," she said to the young mystery searchers with a chuckle, reading the expressions on their faces. "But she's older. And I've been here longer. Just go on back."

The foursome trooped down the hallway.

"Come on in and grab a seat," Leslie said, peering at them over her glasses. She hadn't made a dent in the stacks of papers before her. "I presume you have something to tell me."

"Yes, we do," Tom said. "But first, a question. Have you received anything from the Arizona Corporation Commission in the past month?"

"Not that I can think of. June is not when they contact us—the annual reports aren't due until early next year. Why do you ask?"

Suzanne briefly explained the team's hypothesis regarding the missed notification.

"Well, well," Leslie snapped. Her voice went cold. "That explains the thefts—of the mail, and of Old Blue Dog. I'd like to get my hands around Marsden's neck. *Just once.*"

Pete asked, "Ever hear of Robert Harman Maxwell?"

"No, should I have?" Leslie said, bristling without a sideways glance. It was obvious the thefts had rattled her.

"He's a buddy of Marsden's from university."

"I feel sorry for him."

"And he ended up at the graveyard," Kathy said.

"'At' or 'in?'" Leslie asked with a laugh. She turned toward them once more. "There's a difference, you know."

All four of the young detectives contributed to a swift summary of the night's events, including the late-model vehicle's foray into Cemetery Hill.

Surprise crossed Leslie's face. "In the middle of the night?"

"That's what I said," Suzanne replied. "Ever see him before?" She held her cell phone up.

Leslie adjusted her glasses and stared at the image on the screen. "Never. Rather tough-looking, isn't he?"

"It appears they're in business together," Kathy said. "Which is a little surprising. You painted Marsden as a loner."

"Not at all. The little maggot has a partner, and it's someone he knew from the past. Why would that be a surprise? Sure, he swiped a corporate entity that had no assets—why, we don't know yet. But if Old Blue Dog Co. is up and operating, Marsden isn't likely alone. A successful startup takes more than one person."

Leslie paused, her gaze retreating inward. *She's thinking about something in the distant past*, Suzanne thought.

"I'll tell you another thing too," Leslie said. "Anyone visiting a cemetery after midnight is up to no good. I learned that long ago."

Her office went deathly silent.

LATER THE SAME MORNING, THE FOURSOME DROVE NORTH ALONG Willow Creek Road with Kathy behind the wheel.

"This time in daylight," Suzanne said. "No spookiness, right?"

They turned into the access road between the wide-open gates of Cemetery Hill. The Mustang wound its way among shady promenades lined with trees amid an undulating landscape of sunny meadows dotted with gravestones. The cemetery's central mall lay at the center of an immense bowl surrounded on every side by steep hillsides.

"We've never been here," Pete said. "It's *huge.*"

"And old," said Tom, pointing to a gravestone with a weather-worn inscription dating from 1867.

"A hundred and fifty years," Kathy noted. "Give or take."

A handful of buildings—one barn-like structure and a few garages—clustered together on the left side of the mall, partially obscured from view by a throng of eucalyptus trees. Their doors all spilled wide open. A yellow mechanical digger rested on a driveway out front. They spotted a quartet of groundskeepers riding lawn mowers across broad swathes of parklands, twisting and turning around the gravestones, creating a steady hum of activity in the peaceful atmosphere. All the workers sore lime-green vests, making them easy to identify.

A handful of people visited the gravesites of loved ones, alone or in pairs.

Kathy said, "In one way, the place is so beautiful, it takes your breath away. But it's sad too."

"You expect happiness at a graveyard?" her brother said.

"Drop—dead."

That exchange sent the twins into gales of laughter.

A free-standing, single-story reception center loomed ahead. Kathy parked in a designated parking place out front and the four made their way in through double front doors. A tall, slim, well-dressed woman in her twenties greeted them from behind a counter. She had long, flaming-red hair that fell below her shoulders. A nametag on her blouse read HARRIET.

"Good morning," she said, smiling. The receptionist was polished, professional, and friendly. "How can I help you?"

"We're looking for a gravesite," Suzanne answered.

"Sure. The name, please?" Her hands went to a countertop keyboard.

"Philip Marsden," Kathy answered.

The redhead's eyes flickered. The color on her face drained away.

"Philip Marsden," she repeated. *Tap-tap.* "Do you remember the date he died?"

"Sure," Tom replied. "Last month, May the seventh."

At that moment, a UPS driver walked into the reception area. Without saying a word, he dropped three boxes and a large envelope onto the counter before handing a tablet to the receptionist. She paused and signed for the deliveries. The driver rushed away.

"Ah, here we are. Mr. Marsden is in section seven fifty-four, lot two, plot sixteen," Harriet said, surveying the group with her eyes. "I'll point it out on the map." She tore off a sheet from a booklet of maps and drew a line from YOU ARE HERE to the gravesite. The line followed the roadway to the far side of the cemetery, where she drew an X.

They thanked Harriet and jumped back into the car. Kathy was still at the wheel. Pete held the map and called out directions.

"That lady is *tall*," Suzanne said.

"You're not kidding," Kathy replied. "I hope she's finished growing. Or that the WNBA sends a scout out here."

Tom asked, "Anyone look at those packages that came in?" His demeanor didn't change, but his voice sounded... odd.

Suzanne glanced at her brother. "Look at them? Whatever for?"

"The label on the envelope—on top of the boxes—it's addressed to 'Old Blue Dog Co. dba Better Retirement, Inc.'"

A collective gasp.

"Whoa! Wait a sec," Kathy exclaimed. She almost drove off the road. "What the heck does that mean?"

"Clear as day," Tom replied. "Formal and legal too. This is headquarters." He waved his arms theatrically, taking in the immense mall.

"I'll tell you something else," Pete said. "When we mentioned Philip Marden's name, Harriet's face turned color."

Suzanne said, "You spotted that too?"

"What about the other deliveries?" Pete asked. "Who were they addressed to?"

Tom grinned. "I couldn't very well drill down on that pile. I don't have x-ray vision. Not yet anyway."

Soon, Kathy pulled the Mustang over to the side of the road. Philip Marsden's plot was a short, quiet walk away past a row of three new gravesites. A pungent smell of fresh-cut grass filled the air. Multitudes of birds screeched and tweeted in a never-ending cacophony. The foursome halted at a leafy tree that wasn't even four feet tall. Close to it was a flat gray headstone inscribed Philip Edward Marsden in block letters, together with his birth and death dates. Beneath that appeared the words *Gone but never forgotten*.

"That's weird too," Tom said, pushing his hair back from his forehead.

"Define weird," said Suzanne.

"He had no family."

"You're right," Pete said. "Who would remember him?"

"You just did."

Suzanne said, "Maybe a friend."

"Who knows?"

Pete said, "Detective Ryan was wrong."

Kathy agreed. "Dead wrong."

8

DEMASO'S FUNERAL HOME

The mystery searchers had to convince Prescott City Police to reopen the investigation into Philip Marsden—and whatever was happening on Cemetery Hill.

"It's a must," Suzanne said. "We need their hands on this case—it's *way* beyond us."

"Point taken," Tom said.

That afternoon they returned to the station, huddling with Detective Ryan and the Chief to discuss the mystery's recent twists and turns.

A chagrined Detective Ryan said, "We checked online a month ago, and did everything y'all did—plus contacting the Corporation Commission. There wasn't a set of electronic fingerprints anywhere." He blinked away behind his thin new lenses.

"It all happened in the last three weeks," Tom explained. "Your guys were just early, that's all."

"Well, it's frustrating," the investigator said., "And that UPS package to Old Blue Dog Company proves Leslie's story. It had the dba on it too, huh? What about a return address?"

All eyes focused on Tom. "I didn't notice."

The Chief spoke up. "There's little doubt now that Mr. Marsden *could* be alive. Still, his partner might have ended up with Old Blue Dog Company, and Marsden is dead and buried. That would explain why Maxwell made the post office run."

"No way, Dad," Tom chimed in, polite but firm. "Without Marsden's experience and knowhow, this startup wouldn't go anywhere. He's the leader, we feel certain."

"It's the only thing that makes sense," Suzanne said. "Old Blue Dog is alive and operating on Cemetery Hill, and we've got to figure out where and what's going on."

Silence greeted her words before the Chief spoke again. "It's worth a second look, Joe."

Detective Ryan sighed. "Yup, I'm afraid you're right. Too much evidence, and it's all tied together." He paused. "We'll reopen the investigation."

"Agreed," the Chief said with a chuckle, glancing at his lead investigator. "Appears that Leslie was right."

The detective grinned. "Think of it this way. She won't be mad at us anymore." The two men guffawed.

"Detective Ryan, who did you talk with at DeMaso's Funeral Home?" Suzanne asked.

"Let's see." The investigator dug out a small, handheld notebook from his shirt pocket. He flipped through a few pages. "Aaron DeMaso. He's the funeral director, and he runs the place. A short, dapper guy—well dressed and professional. It's a family business."

The four said their goodbyes. Outside, standing on the sidewalk, they high-fived one another: *Success.*

"Next stop, DeMaso's Funeral Home," Tom said. "It's only a five-minute drive south."

Pete checked the time. "It's late in the afternoon. We'll come back tomorrow if Mr. DeMaso isn't available." He was the gung-ho guy, always ready to roll. Too ready, sometimes. "Why wait?"

Suzanne soon pulled into an almost empty parking lot. Under a sheltering overhang they could see two white hearses.

"No sign of life here," Pete said.

Kathy laughed. "That's funny. No, really."

"Before we go in," Suzanne said, "let's agree. No mention of Old Blue Dog Company or A Better Retirement."

"Good point," Tom said. "Or anything else we know." Suzanne parked out front.

They walked through double glass doors into a giant reception room with high walls and large picture windows, bordered by grass and well-kept flower beds. Light, quiet music played in the background, loud enough without being intrusive. Bunches of flowers engulfed them with a sweet smell. *Carnations,* Suzanne thought. *And roses.* A visitors' book sat on a pedestal, awaiting the next funeral.

A clean-cut man in his mid-twenties with a pale complexion and thinning reddish hair approached them. He wore a neatly pressed dark suit with a white shirt and tie, and his shoes gleamed.

"Good afternoon," he said, greeting them with a friendly smile.

Pete spoke first. "We're looking for Mr. Aaron DeMaso."

"That would be me," the man replied. "My friends call me Aaron. How can I help you?" They could easily imagine him handling bereaved family members with ease.

The four mystery searchers introduced themselves. The funeral director shook hands with them one after another. It turned out he remembered every name. "Great to meet all of you." There was an awkward pause.

Suzanne plunged in. "Aaron, we've just come from meeting with Detective Joe Ryan of the Prescott City Police. You talked to him a week ago."

His eyes narrowed a touch as the smile dropped from his face. "Yes, Suzanne, I did. He asked me about a deceased gentleman. I don't recall his name offhand."

"Philip Marsden," Kathy prompted.

"Ah, yes, quite right. I'm very sorry—are you family?"

"Not at all," Suzanne replied. "His office landlord, Mrs. Leslie McPherson, claims that Mr. Marsden is still alive—that there's been a mistake—a bizarre one too. She asked us to do some research for her."

"Oh, that's interesting." Aaron coughed once. "If you don't mind my asking, why did she ask the four of you, in particular?"

They glanced at one another before Suzanne answered. "We've solved mysteries in the past. Mrs. McPherson had read about us in *The Daily Pilot.*"

The funeral director's face twisted awkwardly—just for a second. "And she thinks Mr. Marsden is alive? That would be a first." There was a quiet, respectful chuckle. "Well, please come in to our family meeting center. Let's see what I can find." He led them to a spacious room with a conference table surrounded by comfortable armchairs upholstered in deep, soft leather. "Make yourself at home. There's coffee here if you'd like it"—he pointed to an adjoining kitchen—"and cold drinks too. I'll fetch Mr. Marsden's file."

"He seems sure of himself," Suzanne whispered as Aaron walked out, barely audible over the soothing music.

"Yes," Kathy agreed. "So confident."

A minute later, he returned with a folder in one hand. He pulled up a large leather chair and joined the young detectives at the conference table.

"I remember Mr. Marsden well," Aaron began. He flipped the file open. "We received his body from the hospital. The poor man died from a rare autoimmune disease. We noted that there was no next of kin." He paused before looking at them. "Mr. Marsden was only twenty-six." He frowned. "He had no friends either. No one showed up to the burial. Always sad whenever that happens."

Kathy asked, "There's an inscription on his gravestone, 'Gone but not forgotten.' Where would that come from?"

"Oh, you visited his gravesite?" DeMaso replied, momentarily taken aback. "Well, we have many such situations—a deceased individual with no family or friends. It's not uncommon. So we use traditional sayings." He paused again, seeming to gather his thoughts. "'Gone but not forgotten' is a favorite of mine."

He passed a document across the table. "Here is Mr. Marsden's final request before he died." Centered on the sheet of writing paper was a single line of crazy, hard-to-read left-handed scrawl, with an illegible signature below it:

After cremation, please bury my remains
in the gravesite I own at Cemetery Hill.

"He had pre-purchased a plot?" Tom asked.

"Yes, two weeks before he passed away—he bought it online, together with his gravestone. Mr. Marsden did not specify what he wanted for his inscription other than his name and life dates, but he paid for the engraving in advance."

"Isn't that rather unusual?" Kathy asked.

"Not at all. Happens all the time."

"Who handles such a purchase?" Pete asked.

"Cemetery Hill," the funeral director replied.

Silence. There was little else to say. It all seemed *normal* under the circumstances. Believable too. The four glanced at one another before pushing their chairs back. Everyone stood and shook hands with Aaron.

"I wish there was something I could do," he said, "but there's no doubt. Philip Marsden died on the seventh of May. Mrs. McPherson —that was her name, right?—can always visit the gravesite to reassure herself." A curious look crossed his face. "I, uh… did wonder, however. Whatever gave her the idea that Mr. Marsden was still alive?"

"Someone stole the antiquated computer he used," Tom replied. "She thought that no one could possibly want it—except Mr. Marsden."

"Oh, I see," Aaron replied, running a hand through his thin hair. He seemed almost relieved. "Well, it's of no use to him now."

"Thanks again," Tom said. "Would you mind if I call you if something else comes up?"

The man's smile returned. "Oh, sure. No problem. I'll get you a business card."

The others said their goodbyes and headed out to the car. Tom followed Aaron into a well-appointed, spacious office. On his desk sat a fountain pen, a yellow pad of paper, and a tiny plexiglass holder for business cards. A large diploma—displayed in a handsome, oversize gilded frame—hung on the wall. Tom's eyes locked on the diploma while Aaron plucked out a single business card.

"There you go, Tom. Please call me anytime. Sorry I couldn't help more."

"Oh, you helped. I can't thank you enough."

"Well, you're welcome." Aaron's eyes flickered as he searched Tom's face. The two shook hands.

Tom stepped out to the car. In fact, he almost *skipped* out. Aaron DeMaso had graduated from the University of Arizona's College of Business.

"Whoa," Pete said after hearing the news. He blinked as he connected the dots. "You're thinking he was a classmate—"

"Of Marsden and Maxwell," Suzanne said, finishing the thought.

"For sure," Tom said, grinning. "I checked the date on the diploma. Aaron DeMaso graduated the same year and from the same class. Those three guys were classmates."

"And best friends, I'd bet," Pete said.

"Friends beyond the grave, even," said Kathy.

9

EMMA BROWN

"So Aaron DeMaso lied," Kathy said. She was at the wheel, piloting the Mustang home.

Tom leaned forward from the backseat. "He sure did. And he lied to the police too."

"A fib is one thing," Suzanne said. "Faking a death and burial takes things to a whole other level. That has to be highly illegal."

"True," Tom agreed. "I'll bet there's a pile of money somewhere. But we have a more immediate problem."

Pete turned and looked at him. "Such as?"

"Think about it. We show up to Cemetery Hill and ask about Philip Marsden. How did the tall lady behind the counter react?"

"Nervous," Kathy recalled.

"Then we stop at DeMaso's Funeral Home. Turns out Aaron DeMaso was classmates with Marsden and Maxwell. But DeMaso pretends he's never heard of the guy."

Suzanne rolled her eyes. "That's a fact. He couldn't even remember his *name*. Okay, I see where you're going."

"It's not good," Tom said with a serious expression. "By now Marsden *knows* someone is on to him. That'll put him on guard."

"And his cronies too," Kathy said. "The whole gang will be on high alert."

"Harriet, DeMaso, Marsden, and Maxwell. That makes four— and there could be others. Business at Old Blue Dog Company is booming." Pete grinned.

"I doubt it," Tom said with a chuckle. "If it was, they wouldn't mess around with McPherson Construction. Five grand isn't a lot of money."

"Unless you don't have any," Suzanne figured.

Kathy knit her brow. "One thing they *do* have is our names."

"Good point," Tom said. "Whatever's up, they've gone to great lengths to protect it. We need to be cautious."

"I'm not liking this," Suzanne said. "Just saying."

"Don't let your imagination run wild," Pete said. "Not yet. First, we'll check out Aaron DeMaso's story."

"That's an easy one," Kathy said.

Pete chortled. "You're thinking the same thing I am."

"You bet I am," his sister replied, winking at her brother. "We'll put Mom on it."

WEDNESDAY MORNING BEGAN WITH AN EARLY PHONE CALL TO LESLIE.

"Based on our findings so far," Suzanne said, "we have evidence that Old Blue Dog Company is operational."

"How reassuring." She paused. "Does this mean Detective Ryan's lights turned back on?"

Tom winced. "Yeah, for sure. The Prescott City Police are reopening the investigation."

"About time," she snapped.

Suzanne shifted the conversation. "Leslie, you mentioned his landlady once. She told you Marsden was dying."

"Uh-huh. He fooled her too. Emma Brown. What about her?"

"We need to talk to her."

"You can find her number online. She lives on Tenth Street."

Then the older woman muttered something unintelligible. Another bad word slipped out before she slammed the phone down without saying goodbye.

Suzanne's eyes were huge. "Wow. She's volatile, that's a fact."

"I'll tell you one thing, she needs a lesson in manners," Tom groused.

The twins looked at each other and burst out laughing.

"She'll never change," Suzanne said.

"Never."

EMMA BROWN RAN A BOARDING HOUSE A FEW BLOCKS EAST OF Whiskey Row, an old Victorian home on the edge of the city's downtown. The girls dropped in early that afternoon.

"Brings back memories," Kathy said as she parked the car. The previous summer they had toured the area just one street away—on the way to solving their memorable second mystery.

Suzanne nodded. Images of the "ghost" in the county courthouse flooded her mind.

Emma Brown turned out to be a plump, middle-aged widow with a blotchy round face, three kids—"They're playing in the backyard"—and two boarders. "To make ends meet," she explained, puckering her lips.

Mrs. Brown wore her hair in a bun and an apron covering her ample girth. After introductions, she invited the girls into a sparse, old-fashioned living room. She insisted on making tea. After a little small talk, her story tumbled out.

"I was sorry to lose Philip," she said. "Such a nice man, and *so* young. Who could ever imagine? Why are you asking now?"

"Well, Mrs. Brown—" Suzanne began.

"Please call me Emma."

"Well, Emma," Kathy said, "Philip worked out of an office at McPherson Construction. Mrs. McPherson, his office landlady, so to speak, believes he still might be alive."

"Good Lord!" Emma exclaimed. She lowered her gaze, her eyes watering. "That horrible woman? Philip told me all about her—always rude and demanding, he said. Imagine that. Doesn't she read the newspaper? The poor man *died*." A tear rolled down her cheek.

A blond-haired boy, who looked to be around ten, raced in, looking for an apple. Emma excused herself and returned a minute later, drying her hands. She sat back down.

Suzanne asked, "Was Philip sick for a long time?"

"Goodness, no," she replied. Her eyebrows shot up. "A month at most. He got worse in the last couple days, fast too. Then, one afternoon when I was out picking up groceries, a friend came and picked him up."

"Where did he go?" Kathy asked.

"Why, to hospice of course. I didn't know which one, otherwise I would have gone to check on the poor man. He never even went to the hospital. Three days later, he died. I never felt so bad." She blew her nose.

The two girls glanced at one another. *A hospice!*

"How do you *know*, Emma?" Suzanne asked. "I mean, who told you?"

"Well, Philip left me a note. Hang on." Emma disappeared for a minute, returning with an envelope. She handed it toward the girls. "Here, see for yourself."

Suzanne extracted a folded sheet of writing paper. Inside—in a jagged, left-handed scrawl—someone had written:

Thank you for everything, Emma.
I'm getting worse—an old school friend is taking me to hospice.
The same friend will return in a few days to pick up my personal effects.
I've enclosed the last $300 I owe you.

All the best,
Philip

"That's Philip Marsden's handwriting," Kathy said, peering over

Suzanne's shoulder. She recognized the style from the note in Aaron DeMaso's file.

"His friend stopped in two days later," Emma continued. "That's when I learned Philip had passed away. Then Philip's obituary appeared in *The Daily Pilot*." She blew her nose again.

"How about the funeral, Emma?" Suzanne asked. "Were you there?"

"Oh, goodness no. It was family only, I was told." She stopped and looked at the girls, wide-eyed. "Do you think I *should* have attended? I mean, it wouldn't have been appropriate, would it?"

"No, you did the right thing," Kathy assured her.

Something clicked in Suzanne's mind. Philip's "friend" had to be the sinister-looking Maxwell—or, maybe more likely, Aaron DeMaso. A search on her cell phone pulled up an image of Maxwell, the one she had taken as he exited the post office.

"Emma, is this the man who picked up Philip's belongings?"

The middle-aged lady reached for a pair of reading glasses from the desk beside her. She adjusted them while scanning the picture. "Goodness, no. I've never seen this man before. He sure looks mean, doesn't he? Besides, Philip's friend was a woman."

"*A woman?*" Suzanne replied, sitting straight up in her chair.

"Oh, yes."

Kathy couldn't believe it. "Do you remember her name?"

Emma stopped. "You know, I don't. But I'll tell you something. She had beautiful red hair. And she was tall."

The girls locked eyes. *Harriet.*

10

PROOF POSITIVE

Heidi Hoover was never the easiest person to pin down.
A few years older than her four friends, Heidi was the star reporter for *The Daily Pilot*. A short, cute young woman with bouncy black curls and a dynamic personality, she lived in the fast lane, racing from one story to another. No matter how often Tom called, she refused to answer her cell phone.

Tom gave up calling and texted her: *Need to meet—dead man walking.*

One hour at corporate, she replied a minute later.

Pete grinned. "See? We know what makes her tick."

"So what's it all about?" Heidi said, greeting the boys as they walked into her narrow office. Her words shot out rapid-fire—not a moment to waste. "Dead man walking?" She giggled. "Funny. Very."

Heidi made them smile. Despite their difference in age, she had turned into a good friend and ally. In their previous case—after they had uncovered the secrets of a mysterious mansion—she had been first on the scene to rescue them from mortal danger. She had shared in the reward too.

The boys brought her up to date.

"Wow, what a story!" the reporter exclaimed. "The guy steals a company and then fakes his own death to throw the police off. Heady stuff, for sure. How can I help?"

"Two things," Tom began. "First, we need access to the newspaper's archives."

"No problem," Heidi said. She jumped up with a quick "Follow me" and led them through a familiar maze of corridors. "You've been here before. What else?"

"Well, if we can't solve the mystery," Tom called out as they hurried down a hallway, "we'll have to smoke Philip out—force him into the open by revealing we know he's still alive."

"Can you prove that?"

"We're positive," Pete said.

"Yeah, but can you *prove* it?"

"Well..." Tom replied with a little hesitation. "Not today, but—"

"That's a 'no,'" Heidi cut in. "Okay. Keep me in the loop. I'll figure something out. Could be a human-interest story. And we already have a title."

"Which is?"

"'*Dead man walking,*'" Heidi said, giggling once more. "You sent it over in your message. What could be better?"

They stepped into the archives' office just as Heidi's cell phone buzzed. "Go for it, I gotta run." She rushed off, shouting back, "Call me if you find anything!"

The boys spent the balance of the afternoon at *The Daily Pilot.* The previous summer, while working on the case of the ghost in the county courthouse, Heidi had shown them how to search the newspaper's archives.

"We save all the stories in the last decade in digital form," she had explained. "We tag each one with keywords. Use this computer to enter a subject. If there's a match, the system will pull up specific headlines and matching dates. If you find something interesting, hit *Print.*"

The boys began with Philip Marsden's name. The entry pulled up his obituary notice, nothing else.

"Try Aaron DeMaso," Tom suggested. That name, tied to DeMaso's Funeral Home, disgorged a countless number of puff stories on the business but little about the man himself. Keying in DeMaso Funeral Home brought up dozens more articles, the majority linking to a specific deceased individual.

Sometime later, Suzanne and Kathy rushed in, excited to share their news. The details of their afternoon meeting with Emma Brown tumbled out.

"So Harriet picked him up," Tom said. "Go figure."

"Big surprise, huh?" his sister replied. "How are those two connected?"

"Aaron DeMaso, I'd guess," Kathy said.

"Okay, we're down to the last search," Pete said. He typed in *Cemetery Hill.* The foursome waded through hundreds of obituary notices, some dating back decades.

An hour later, starving hungry and ready to quit, Pete sat up and yelled, "Bingo!"

"What is it?" his sister cried out. "What did you find?"

Pete touched *Print.* "A charitable group known as the Roper Ranch Family Foundation donated the land on the northern ridgeline overlooking the grassy mall... let's see... three months ago. It seems the cemetery's available supply of land had dwindled. They needed more room for new burials. The generous gift came with a century-old ranch house."

His eyes blazed. "Guess what happened to that house?" He answered his own question before anyone else had a chance. "They rented it out! For two years—while they prepare the land that will become part of the cemetery."

"Nice," Suzanne said.

"You bet," Tom said. "So along came Old Blue Dog Company."

"It sure did," Kathy said, pumping her arm into the air. "They stepped right in and rented it."

Suzanne's mind blipped. "*Wait*—I don't recall seeing a house on a hill out there."

"Me neither," Kathy said.

"We weren't looking up," Pete said. "It's a haul to the top. And there's no graveyard there. Not yet."

Suzanne opened Google Earth and located Cemetery Hill. She changed the view to see the north ridge and silently studied the scene for a few moments. Then, "Check it out."

In the angled image, almost but not quite straight down, they could see an old-looking house with a shingled roof, apparently only one story high, perched on top of a flat ridge, bare but for three trees. The ranch house faced due north and backed up to an overview of the cemetery. On the west side appeared a broad graveled lot with parking for half a dozen vehicles: empty. A tiny structure showed to the east—a shed or something similar, closer to the ridgeline. A winding gravel artery led a mile north before merging onto Willow Creek Road. Another road, steep and narrow, ran straight down the hill and merged with Cemetery Hill's circular roadway through an access gate.

"So if you're driving between Prescott and the Roper family ranch the shortest distance by far is through Cemetery Hill," Tom said. "Makes perfect sense. They owned the house *and* the hillside down to the graveyard's old property line."

Kathy's cell phone rang. She put the call on speaker. "Hi, Mom. Any luck?"

"Depends on how you look at it," Maria replied, her voice fading in and out as she buzzed around the hospital. "There's no record of a Philip Marsden registering. I checked with Emergency, Intensive Care, and Palliative Care too. They've never heard of him." She sounded breathless but seemed to enjoy playing a key role in their latest investigation.

"So much for Aaron DeMaso's story," Pete said.

"That jibes with what Marsden's landlady told us," said Suzanne.

56

"She said he went directly to hospice, never even set foot in a hospital."

"Well," said Maria, "if he ended up there, he didn't go into the public facility affiliated with our hospital. I checked that too."

"What if a person never gets to hospice and *dies* at Prescott Regional?" Pete asked. "There would be a record there, right?"

"Oh, sure," she replied. "Two people died here during the first week of May—but neither one was Philip Marsden." Then she laughed, a loud laugh that sounded charmingly like her daughter's. "You can't check out if you never check in!"

Maria disconnected into a collective silence.

Suzanne spoke first. "Now what?"

"Now we have proof positive," Tom said. "It was all faked, to stop any investigation into the thefts from MacPherson Construction. There was no 'rare autoimmune disease.'"

"Right," Pete said. "and I'm betting there was no hospice either. It was all part of a ruse."

"Maybe so," Suzanne put in, "but that still leaves the question: how did he manage to fake his own *death*?"

Kathy pictured the funeral director as she replayed his words in her mind. "Aaron DeMaso, of course. Do you realize how many lies that man told? He..." She shook her head. What else was there to say?

Suzanne messaged Heidi Hoover with an update, ending with a big *Thank you!*

"Okay," Tom said. "I think our next move is obvious."

11

A HILLSIDE SURVEY

They drew lots, Pete won—and couldn't stop grinning. *That* bugged his sister to no end.

"No gloating," Kathy admonished him sternly.

Suzanne came in second. For a few moments, she avoided eye contact with her best friend. After losing to her brother, Kathy was in a foul mood.

"Don't sweat it," Tom said, trying to cheer her up. "We'll hide out down here and guard the road."

"Big deal."

It was after ten o'clock on Wednesday night, a cool and breezy summer evening in Prescott. Tom was at the wheel of the Chevy, cruising along Cemetery Hill's circular roadway, lights off. The grassy mall slipped past by in slow motion.

The goal was to survey the house on the ridge. Thinking ahead and not knowing what to expect, the foursome had dressed in dark clothes. In the back of their minds, caution was the keyword.

"Remember," Tom warned earlier, "Marsden is carrying a weapon."

Now, it was showtime.

"You realize how freaky this is, right?" Suzanne asked as the

Chevy circled the grassy mall. "We're the only ones out here—the only *live* ones, anyway."

"I sure hope so," Kathy said, studying the gravesites as they passed by.

They stopped shy of the ranch house's open gate and the steep road leading to the top of the ridge.

"Okay," Tom said. "Remember, if we call or message, it means that another car has showed up, and it's heading up the hill."

"Got it," Pete said. This was *way* too much fun. He almost saluted.

"Good luck."

"Yes, sir," Suzanne said, mocking her brother.

Suzanne and Pete stepped from the car, gazing up. From the bottom of the hill, only the roof of the ranch house was visible, shrouded by a soft glow of light.

"Oh, boy," Pete said, rubbing his hands together. "This should be interesting."

Suzanne, careful by nature, felt a little trepidation. "Let's not get caught."

"I hadn't planned on it."

"Good to hear."

By prior agreement, Tom drove the Chevy farther along the mall's circular road, then turned around for an unobstructed view of the grassy mall, the hillside, and the gravel road leading up to the ranch house. From this vantage point, he and Kathy could spot an incoming car on Cemetery Hill's roadway, long before it reached the gate. He pulled over, shut off the ignition, and opened the windows.

"Can you see anything?" he asked Kathy.

"Not a thing," she replied. "Way too dark."

Pete and Suzanne began their trek upwards. Somewhere in the distance, the *whooo-whooo* of an owl started. Except for the ever-present cicadas, the steep hillside was quiet, the only sound falling footsteps on the rough graveled road. Five minutes passed before they paused, catching their breath.

"We're close," Pete said, breathing hard. He loved every second of the adventure.

Not much later, they caught the whiff of an odd smell. "What is that?" Suzanne whispered.

"Cigarette smoke, I think."

"Awful."

Then they froze. Faint voices carried on the breeze. Car doors slammed, and an ignition fired up. Then two more. There was a distinct sound of tires rolling on gravel.

"Get off the road!" Suzanne hissed.

They raced across the hillside, ducking low, putting distance between themselves and the roadway. A vehicle's headlights bounced as the car negotiated its way down the hill.

"Hit the ground!" Pete warned hoarsely. They buried themselves into wild grass, their eyes searching. A second vehicle appeared, and a third.

"Check it out," Suzanne whispered. "It's a convoy."

"Must be Miller time," Pete quipped.

The first car halted, parallel to their prone bodies and only a few yards away. A man jumped out from the front passenger seat and walked back and forth, scanning the hillside.

Pete and Suzanne hugged the ground, hoping that the tall grass and their dark clothes sheltered them in the night.

Two other cars stopped.

"What's going on?" someone yelled out.

"There's something moving out here."

"Was is a fox?"

"No—larger. Two, I'd swear."

"People have spotted bears out here."

"Well, whatever. They're long gone now."

A murmur of voices followed, then laughter. Car doors slammed again. Tires crunched on the gravel again as the vehicles passed by. *Too dark to see inside them.* The shrill sound of a million cicadas filled the night once more.

"That was fun," Pete said, standing up. He held a hand out to Suzanne.

"That was *close*," she replied softly. "And it wasn't fun at all." Her heart hammered. She stood and pulled out her cell phone.

"You okay?" Tom asked as he answered. "Three vehicles passed us and left the grounds. There were two passengers in each car."

"Yeah, we're fine. And we avoided them. Just wanted you to know."

"Okay. The lights are still on up there."

"On our way."

Pete and Suzanne halted at the ridgeline, waiting in silence to gather their bearings. Before them loomed the ranch house, its lights mostly extinguished. The back door opened. A man stepped outside and paused, looking around, cloaked in darkness. A match flared as he lit a cigarette.

He puffed away for a couple minutes, never moving from the back step. Then he threw the cigarette to the ground and crushed it. The door closed; the light faded. Suzanne's heartbeat slowed.

———————

THE CHIEF HEARD THE TWINS RETURN AT MIDNIGHT. HE SLIPPED INTO the kitchen and put on a pot of coffee.

"Hi, Dad." Surprised to see her father, Suzanne gave him a hug. "You didn't have to wait up for us."

"Uh-huh," the Chief said, pulling out three empty cups from the cupboard. "Fill me in."

Sherri padded in, yawning and pulling on her housecoat. "You're not having all this fun without me." Tom grabbed another empty cup and set it on the table.

Revelations spilled out across the kitchen table: Emma Brown and her visit from Harriet; Philip Marsden faking his own death; Aaron DeMaso's litany of lies and deceptions; and Old Blue Dog Company's revival on the ridgeline at Cemetery Hill. At one point, their father located a yellow pad and took copious notes. Tom poured the coffee.

"You couldn't see his face?" the Chief asked.

"Way too dark," Suzanne replied.

"Okay. So the guy went back in the house," he reiterated. "What did you do then?"

"Well, the last light shut off," Suzanne replied. She sipped the hot coffee, which was delicious, with loads of cream. "Nothing to see. We made our way down the hill."

"Kathy and I were watching," Tom hurried to add, reading the expression on his mother's face. "Keeping an eye on them, just in case."

The Chief smiled to himself. His twins planned to follow his path into law enforcement, which delighted him to no end. "Yeah, you need to be *really* careful—please. Meanwhile, I've got something for you."

"What is it?" Tom asked, sitting straight up.

"Remember the UPS package to Old Blue Dog Company?"

"Yes!" the twins replied.

"Detective Ryan tracked it down to a Swiss bank. Mr. Marsden is up to his old tricks."

Tom focused. "He's running another scam, and the money's heading to Switzerland. We were right—a technology startup."

"I agree," the Chief said. "You guys have stumbled onto quite a story."

"Well, Heidi will be overjoyed," Tom said. "But it doesn't explain why they robbed Leslie."

"Maybe the cash wasn't rolling in yet," Sherri said, thinking out loud.

"That's possible," the Chief replied. He glanced over at the twins. "Detective Ryan could show up there, asking questions. The problem is that we could make things worse—they'd shut down and set up shop elsewhere. We need proof."

"We're trying out best," Tom said.

"I wonder if you can get pictures of the cars going up that hill?"

The twins looked at each other. "Yeah, we can do that," Tom said.

"The occupants too," the Chief added. "And don't forget the license plates—the most important thing."

"We'll put up a drone too," Suzanne said. "At night, while they're working. Safer than slipping up there."

"All of this is making me nervous," Sherri said, sipping her hot coffee. She held the cup with both hands, shielding her face. Only her worried eyes showed above the rim.

"We're always careful, Mom. Don't worry," Suzanne said, giving her a hug.

"It's okay," Tom assured his mother. "We split into teams and guard one another. And we all carry cell phones."

She blanched. "*Cell phones?* What good does that do? At least one of those guys carries a gun!"

12

"HELLO, PHILIP"

"There they are," Pete said, pointing to a line of lime-green vests hanging inside the barn-like structure.

Tom stared through the windshield from behind the wheel of the Chevy. "Is the place empty?"

"Yup, not a soul. Pull in closer."

It was nine o'clock on Thursday morning when their car ground to a stop before the giant, wide-open doors. Inside, on the left-hand wall, the vests hung on a lengthy line of wooden pegs. There were gaps like missing teeth where workers had plucked a few.

Groundskeepers had deployed across the grassy mall. The sound of a multiple riding lawn mowers filled the air, and the smell of cut grass wafted into the Chevy's cabin. In the distance, on the far side of the mall, a noisy mechanical digger excavated fresh gravesites. Every worker wore a bright lime-green vest with reflective patches.

Pete jumped out and slipped into the barn. He returned with two vests hidden under his jacket. "Okay, let's go," he said with a broad grin as he leaped into the front passenger seat. "We'll return them later."

Tom backed away and merged onto the mall's circular roadway.

The boys had an early start that morning, arriving at Ray's by eight to pick up the hardware. Their plan was to install a hidden high-speed camera at the base of the hill, pointing toward the gate. The mystery searchers had used the system on previous cases, transferring images to their phones over the Internet.

The results were stellar, but in recent times the school's technology club had experimented with motion detectors, adding a wireless detector.

"It'll trigger from up to a hundred feet away," Tom explained. "We can program it to fire off half a dozen frames in rapid sequence and upload to the Cloud."

Their target was vehicles coming and going through the gate. "Car and occupants first," Tom had advised Pete. "Then, on day two, we'll flip the camera around and get rear license plates."

The boys parked at a distance, donned the green vests—they pretended to be greenkeepers—and walked to the target area with a box full of equipment.

"Like we're working on the underground sprinklers," Pete said. He chortled.

"That's the idea."

They worked quickly, attaching a tiny wireless motion detector to one gatepost. Then, a few dozen yards farther along the circular roadway, they located a tree that would serve their purposes. Tom climbed into the branches, strategically locating the camera and locking it down with wire. Viewed from the ground, it was invisible behind the summer greenery.

"Okay," Tom said, breathing hard as he jumped down. "Drive over to the gate. The camera will take a burst of six shots, then transfer them to the Cloud and onto my cell phone app. I'll wait on the mall."

Pete started along the mall's circular roadway. Tom crossed over into the grassy area, disappearing behind old raised gravestones. No sooner had he positioned himself before a late-model Nissan appeared. Pete hurried back.

"Look familiar?" he asked.

"Very."

The vehicle turned left and lumbered up the hill before vanishing over the ridgeline. The boys sat down on the grass, waiting, eyes on the app. A minute later, Tom's cell phone lit up.

"Here they come," Tom said. Pete whistled.

The six shots appeared, one after another—front and side views of the car, plus a clear shot of the driver in images two and three: a tough-looking man, with sunglasses and a pockmarked face.

The boys recognized him. *"Maxwell."*

JUST AFTER NINE THAT EVENING, KATHY PULLED OFF THE ROADWAY and parked the Mustang on the far side of the grassy mall. The foursome dragged a large aluminum case from the trunk. Then, kneeling in the grass, they unpacked the sophisticated drone.

They used their cell phone flashlights as discreetly as possible, assembling the wings and locking them down—tight. Flying time was half an hour without recharging, but the mystery searchers had figured five minutes would be plenty.

Kathy searched a moonless sky. "Perfect weather."

Pete whooped, "Let her rip!"

The drone lifted off with a soft whirring sound. Suzanne piloted the aircraft into the darkness. By federal law, drones could fly to a maximum height of four hundred feet—but tonight this one would fly lower. Much lower.

Tom said, "Bring it in high and circle the ranch house."

"And make sure no one's wandering around outside," Kathy advised.

The high-def camera displayed images on their cell phone apps, but Suzanne tracked everything on the controller's built-in screen. Visibility in the darkness was close to zero. Seconds later, the drone crested the ridgeline and shot up, surveying the ranch house from a respectful distance. Light poured from every window.

Four vehicles parked on the gravel. An attached garage appeared to the left. A stand-alone shed stood to the right.

"Pull to the left side," Pete said, his voice clipped. "There's more light. That's it…way back."

Suzanne sent the drone two hundred feet west and allowed it to descend. "One hundred…ninety… eighty…"

"Whoa," Tom exclaimed. "Look—at—that."

The drone hovered, stationary, with a straight-line view into the garage through its open door. Inside were four computer stations with monitors, each one manned.

"The guy at the back is Maxwell," Kathy said.

"You're right," Suzanne said.

"They're all programmers," Tom muttered. That didn't surprise him—coders were the people who made technology startups possible.

One man, wearing a baseball cap, pushed a chair sideways and stood—he was on the shorter side—and wandered around the garage, his back to the camera. Papers in hand, he stepped from one station to another. A brief conversation took place. The man turned and ambled into the night.

"Move in closer," Kathy prompted.

Suzanne pushed the drone forward, but only so far.

"Remember what happened on Apache Canyon Drive," she warned. There, the drone's wing had caught a last ray of the setting sun, and the reflection had divulged their presence.

The man pivoted, left to right. His handsome profile appeared in sharp relief against the garage. A tiny burst of light flared as he lit a dangling cigarette. He blew smoke out from the corner of his mouth and watched a light breeze whisk it away. He looked up at the night sky before pulling off his cap with his free hand and placed it under his other arm. Then he ran his fingers through blond hair.

"Hello, Philip," Suzanne whispered as she caught her breath.

THE HOUSE ON CEMETERY HILL

On Friday morning, *The Daily Pilot* ran a photograph of Philip Edward Marsden on the front page. It was the same shot Detective Ryan had shown days earlier, minus the stamp of FLORENCE STATE PRISON and Marsden's prison number.

The caption read, "Have you seen this man? Please contact Detective Joe Ryan at Prescott City Police." A phone number ran beside it.

"Very nice," Suzanne said at the breakfast table. She cracked open a hard-boiled egg. "This will put serious heat on those guys at Cemetery Hill."

The twins messaged Detective Ryan, requesting a meeting. Just after ten o'clock, the foursome walked into a large conference room at police headquarters. The detective was waiting for them, coffee cup in hand, a case file open before him. Moments later, the Chief arrived.

"Did you see the newspaper this morning?" the investigator asked, scanning their faces. There was a soft collective murmur.

"Any responses yet?" Tom asked.

"Yup, just one, first thing," the detective reported. "An emotional Emma Brown. It took a bit to calm her down."

"Oh, of course," Suzanne said, "Poor Emma."

"There'll be more," the Chief said. "Your friend, Heidi, really came through. She persuaded her editor to give us an excellent position on the front page, didn't she?"

Thursday's dramatic events spilled out. Suzanne played back the footage—and the evening's startling conclusion—on her cell phone to the entranced police officers.

"Good work," Detective Ryan exclaimed. "I mean, this is great."

"Well, that's our guy," the Chief said, grinning like a schoolboy. "He sure looks healthy."

"Yeah, not bad for a dead guy," the detective said. The two men chuckled.

"We can't tell what they're up to, can we?" the Chief asked.

"Not yet," Tom replied. "And we haven't captured shots of the license plates. We're going back out there today to turn the camera around."

Three vehicles had made the hillside journey the previous afternoon, one person per car, no passengers.

"Contractors, I bet." Tom said. "Programmers hired to write code."

"Both Marsden and Maxwell were coding too," Pete said.

"You'd never pick Maxwell for a programmer," Kathy commented.

"Well, looks are often deceiving," Detective Ryan. "He's a crack coder and a suspect in the Tucson heist. But the authorities couldn't prove it."

The Chief rubbed his chin. "Do we have enough evidence to shut them down?"

"Yes, we do," the detective replied. "We can charge Robert Maxwell for the theft of fifty-two hundred dollars, *after* Leslie makes a complaint—she refuses to return my phone calls. And now there's proof Philip Marsden stole Old Blue Dog Company. But those are minor charges. I'd like to nail them for the startup. Whatever they're doing at the house on Cemetery Hill, it's big. But we need evidence."

"Well, what's your next move?" the Chief asked, looking at the foursome.

"We're not sure," Tom replied. "One option is to bug the garage."

"I'd rather you didn't," the Chief warned. "Too dangerous."

"I agree," Detective Ryan said. "Philip Marsden has a bad habit of going crazy if he doesn't get his way."

LATER, THE GIRLS STOPPED IN TO SEE LESLIE, ANXIOUS TO PLAY THE drone's video for her.

"You're gonna love this," Suzanne said.

"I can't wait," Leslie replied. She adjusted her reading glasses before the trio watched, in utter silence, as the drone circled the house on Cemetery Hill.

Something caused Leslie to gasp out loud. Her eyes watered, and her face appeared to sag. For the first time since they had known her, she looked her age. Then the shot focused in on Marsden, his profile appearing in sharp relief.

"That little maggot," she muttered, her expression darkening.

The girls glanced at each other. They had expected Leslie to react joyfully to the video. Instead, a disturbing gloom had instantly settled over her.

"Someone donated the ranch to Cemetery Hill," Suzanne explained, speaking in a bright tone and trying to lift Leslie's spirits. "The land it stands on is the next phase of the graveyard's development."

"The planning will take two years," Kathy said. "In the meantime, the board of Cemetery Hill rented the home out..."

"To Old Blue Dog Company," Suzanne said, picking up the thread, "and your old friend, Philip Marsden."

Depression had settled over Leslie like a wet blanket. "That little rat is doing everything in his power to spite me. What are those computer people doing?"

"No clue," Kathy replied. She rushed to add, "But we'll figure it out."

Leslie said a bad word and sank deeper in her chair.

MEANWHILE, THE BOYS RETURNED TO CEMETERY HILL AND DONNED the green vests they had borrowed. Once again, Tom parked a distance from the hillside gate and they walked along the main circular roadway.

At one point, a car passed with two passengers in the front seat. It turned onto the gravel road and headed up the hill. The occupants didn't give the boys a second glance.

Pete chuckled. "Boy, these vests are something else, aren't they? They'll protect us from kryptonite." They laughed.

Tom climbed back into the tree. Minutes later, with the reversed camera locked into place, they hustled over to the Chevy and headed out.

Images popped up on Tom's app until 5:00 p.m. As each license plate photo arrived, Tom forwarded it to Detective Ryan.

An hour later, the four mystery searchers caught up with one another at their favorite meeting place. Over ice-cold teas at the Shake Shack, the boys didn't have much to report—"Except the kryptonite-free zone," Pete drew a few laughs. But the girls' encounter with Leslie was the topic of conversation.

"Then she hammered her desk again," Suzanne said, explaining Leslie's unexpected behavior. "And her language turned bad. That woman is something else."

"I thought she'd have a heart attack," Kathy said. "I mean, it flipped her right out! Marsden bothers her to no end."

"I don't understand," Tom said. "It confirmed everything she believed about the case. What's not to like?"

THAT EVENING, THE CHIEF ATTENDED A MEETING IN PHOENIX. THE twins shared dinner with their mother, who sat through a retelling of the day's events.

"Well, isn't that—" Sherri began.

Suzanne's cell phone rang. "Unknown Caller." She answered in her typical warm manner. "Hi, this is Suzanne."

A vaguely familiar voice piped up in the background. "It's Pat, Leslie's secretary."

"Oh, hi, Pat." A warning bell went off in Suzanne's head. The woman hadn't ever called before. "How can I help you?"

"I'm worried about Leslie."

"Worried? What's wrong." She put the call on speaker.

"After you left this afternoon, Leslie became enraged. No matter what I said, she refused to calm down. She quit work early and slammed the door behind her. Now she refuses to answer her cell phone." Pat sounded upset. She seemed to be pacing around agitatedly, with her phone on speaker—her voice faded in and out. "I'm concerned for her safety."

Suzanne said, "I—I don't understand. Whatever has she done?"

Seconds ticked by before Pat replied. It was as if she didn't want to speak the words. "I think she drove out to the ranch... to confront Philip Marsden."

"What?" Suzanne blurted out. "To the house on Cemetery Hill? I hope you're kidding."

"I wish I was," Pat replied. "When you stopped by and gave her the news, she became unhinged. I couldn't talk sense into her."

"Well," Suzanne said, "we realized that we had upset her, but this is a huge turn of events. It could even be dangerous! I mean, sure, Marsden is alive, but no one expected him *not* to be!"

Tom spoke up. "When you say 'news,' Pat, what upset her? What triggered Leslie?"

"What triggered her," Pat replied in a troubled voice, "is that Leslie grew up on that ranch. The house on Cemetery Hill was her family home. And Philip knew it."

14

CAPTURED

"Suzie, we've gotta get out there," Tom said, grabbing the keys.

His sister hurried behind him, still talking on her phone. "Pat, no one ever mentioned Leslie's connection to the ranch house."

"Not even Leslie," Tom said.

"Be careful!" Sherri yelled as her twins raced to the garage.

"We will!" Tom shouted in reply.

"Well," Pat replied, "she didn't want people to know. Leslie's a very generous person, and private too."

Suzanne recalled the newspaper article in *The Daily Pilot*. "A charitable foundation donated the land."

"Her parents set up the Roper Ranch Family Foundation," Pat said, "before they died. Everything passed to Leslie. Roper was her maiden name."

"Why didn't she *tell* us?" Suzanne shook her head. "Okay, got it. We're on our way. I'll call you when we know something."

The twins jumped into the Chevy and headed north with Tom at the wheel. Suzanne messaged the Brunellis with the shocking news.

Kathy replied, *On r way.*

It was after seven, and the setting sun glowed on the horizon. Since the Brunellis lived farther north, they led the way in their

Mustang Hatchback. The twins caught up with the siblings on Willow Creek Road just before the entrance to Cemetery Hill. The two vehicles cranked right, driving through the looming wrought-iron gates and onto the circular roadway. A minute later, they pulled up to the grassy mall, short of the hillside gate.

The four of them stepped out of their cars. The sun had set. They were alone—not another vehicle within sight. A pervasive quietness had settled on the mall.

"What's the plan?" Pete asked, rubbing his hands in glee. He loved adventure.

"It's not your turn, buddy," Kathy said, poking him in the side. "Tom and I are going up."

"What?"

"Let's go, Tom! There's no time to waste."

Kathy made Suzanne laugh. "We'll guard down here," she said.

Pete grumbled, but he knew his sister was right. "Okay, keep your cell phones handy. Who knows what's up there?"

"Leslie, we hope," Kathy quipped.

"Better move the cars farther away," Tom suggested, handing over his keys.

"Will do."

Tom and Kathy tackled the deathly quiet hillside. They caught their breath halfway up and kept going. It wasn't long before they reached the ridgeline and peeked over—nervous and breathing hard—into total bedlam. They had arrived toward the left side of the back of the ranch house, close to the open garage. There was movement—lots of it—as people rushed around. Loud voices shouted. Doors slammed. A man swore.

"Look, they're getting out of Dodge," Kathy hissed. It was obvious: the technology team was packing up for a move.

"I think you're right," Tom whispered. "Leslie must have spooked them big time."

"What should we do?"

Tom's mind raced. "Let's slide along the ridgeline that way." He pointed right. "Too many people here."

"Okay," Kathy whispered. "Leslie's gotta be close by."

The two slipped further along. Moments later, they poked their heads up again. The noise level had dropped off as they reached the far corner of the house. The shed was a few yards farther but closer to the ridgeline.

"I hope they don't see us," Kathy whispered.

"Well, no one's here now. Let's go!"

The two scaled the brow of the ridge and raced to the house. The right side bedrooms blazed with lights. Tom stretched up and peeked in through a window.

A woman's voice called out, just barely audible, *"I'm over here!"*

"What the—"

The two looked at each other.

"Where did that voice come from?" Kathy whispered.

"Behind you!" Leslie hollered again. They heard the unmistakable sound of fists hammering on wood.

"That's her," Tom said, stifling a smile. He'd recognize that voice anywhere.

"She's in the shed!" Kathy whispered as she turned around.

They hurried over to the structure which, close up, proved to be built from thick, old, unpainted planks. They could see one of Leslie's fingers sticking out from a narrow crack between the door and the doorframe.

"About time," the older woman growled. "Didn't you hear me?"

The last glow of the setting sun glinted off a metal chain that wrapped round the door latch, secured by a huge steel lock. *Uh-oh.*

"Leslie," Tom said in a low, hoarse voice. "How can we free you?"

At that moment, he started as something hard poked into his back.

"You can't. Hands up!" Two flashlight beams clicked on, sweeping the area around the shed, pointing into the faces of the captured searchers.

"Leave them alone!" Leslie shrieked from inside.

"Shut up, you old goat!" a man's voice shouted.

Tom and Kathy, blinded by the powerful flashlights, felt guns pushed into their bellies. *Philip Marsden and Robert Maxwell,* they realized with a sense of dread.

"Two of the kids that tracked us," one man snarled. As the beams of light splashed around, Tom and Kathy recognized Maxwell.

"Who are you?" he demanded. "What are you doing here?"

"Leave them be!" Leslie shouted. "They're friends of mine."

"Your miserable old hag," the other man retorted. *Marsden.* "You're the one that caused all the trouble." He slammed the side of the shed with his flashlight.

"You are nothing but a maggot!" Leslie retorted, hammering on the inside wall with her fist.

Boy, Kathy thought, *this is one feisty lady.*

"Cell phones!" the man demanded. Up close, their eyes adjusting to the light, they both recognized Marsden's distinctive face. He jammed his flashlight under one arm and held out an open hand, raising his gun with the other. Leslie's words from the past tore through Tom's mind: *The man went into a rage... I had no idea how dangerous he was.*

"Hand them over, now!" Marsden snapped, seething and talking through his teeth. He ripped their cell phones from their hands and tossed them onto the ground.

Meanwhile, Maxwell had removed the lock. He pulled away the chain with a loud metallic rattling sound and yanked the door open, its hinges squealing. Leslie surged forward, shouting, but Maxwell gave the older woman a heavy shove. Then he grabbed Kathy by her ponytail and pitched her in, screaming and head first, onto the wooden floor.

Marsden gave Tom a solid, unexpected kick. He stumbled as something slammed down against the back of his head.

He fell hard. Everything turned black.

15

SHELTER FROM THE STORM

"*What was that?*" Suzanne cried.

"A woman screamed," Pete said. "I—look, *flashlights!*"

They stared up to the ridgeline. Beams of light arced from the ranch house, across the ridge, bouncing erratically.

"Uh-oh," Suzanne said. "I hope that wasn't Kathy."

"We gotta get up there," Pete shouted. "Quick."

They charged along a now familiar route much faster than the first time they had climbed up to the ridge. Minutes later, they not quite crested the hill when a voice came out of nowhere.

"Can I help you?"

Suzanne felt as if her hair stood on end. A chill ran up her back. The startled duo froze. Their breath came in gasps, putting them at a disadvantage.

"Who are you?" Pete managed to ask.

A man stepped toward them out of the darkness. In one hand, he held a handgun pointed toward them; in the other, a flashlight that he clicked on, pointing eerily upward from his chin and across his face. *Maxwell.*

"Makes no difference who I am, but I gather you're here to check on your friends." His tone changed. "Follow the gravel road to the ridgeline. *Now!*"

No choice. They trudged along, worried. Just as they bridged the top, Maxwell shouted out, "Philip!" A second man ran up in the dark and another flashlight clicked on, blinding them. *Marsden.* Pete and Suzanne halted, silent and still.

"We've been expecting you." Marsden walked over and whacked Pete on the head with his flashlight.

"Leave him alone!" Suzanne cried, fear and anger flooding her in equal measures. Up close, she recognized his face. It had turned ugly.

He ignored her. The two men shoved the sluggish couple toward the shed, Pete stumbling and moaning, clutching his head with both hands. "Unlock the door, Robert."

Pete's fingers felt sticky and wet. Maxwell hauled the noisy chain out and flung open the door. This time no one inside moved.

"Gimme your cell phones!" Marsden bellowed. He smashed the phones out of their hands with his flashlight, slamming the devices onto the gravel. An unexpected kick propelled Suzanne into the shed. Maxwell hammered Pete's head with the butt of his revolver and tossed him into the darkened space.

Pete reeled and fell into his sister's arms. The door slammed.

"You okay, buddy?" Tom asked, grabbing his shoulder.

It took moments for words to form in Pete's mind. "Yeah... I'm okay. I've... got a terrific headache."

Tom grimaced, unseen, in the dark. "Join the club."

"Oh, Pete, thank goodness," Kathy said. Just thinking about the stickiness of fresh blood as it dried always made her sick, even when she couldn't see it. She dabbed his head with her shirt sleeve.

Pete grinned to himself. "That I've got a headache?"

Kathy punched her brother gently.

"Well, well," Leslie said. "The gang's all here."

Tom wobbled to his feet.

"No sense getting up," Suzanne said. "You're not going anywhere."

"No fooling," he replied. "I'm trying to find my bearings."

Leslie spoke. "You're in the shed my father built." She hesitated. "My temper got the better of me. I'm sorry I landed you into this mess."

That's a first, Tom thought. But his heart went out to her. "No problem, Leslie. We all make mistakes. Why didn't you tell us?"

"Some things are confidential, that's why." Her voice cracked.

Suzanne touched Leslie's arm. "We'll get out of this, I'm sure." But it was bad, she realized. *Really bad.*

"How did they catch you?" Pete asked the older woman.

"Well," Leslie replied, "when I drove up, they were working in the garage. By the time I parked, Philip Marsden was standing there with his arms folded, waiting for me. He dragged me out of the car and over to the shed. And he whacked me twice just for fun."

Outraged, Suzanne said, "Imagine hitting a seventy-year-old woman!"

Leslie smiled to herself. "Thank you, dear. I'm closer to eighty, but I do appreciate the compliment." She chuckled. "Anyway, two hours later I spotted Tom and Kathy through a gap in the plank wall. I shouted out a warning, but the rest is history."

"Any idea what these guys are doing?" Kathy asked.

"Not yet," Tom said with an unseen grimace. "But when we showed up, it appeared the technology team was moving out."

"That photo in the newspaper had to freak Marsden right out," Suzanne said.

"Well, that makes sense," Pete said, nodding. "Then you showed up, Leslie, and spooked them even more. That put them over the edge."

Leslie chuckled quietly. "Zeke would say it served me right."

Tom sat down again. Inside the shed, it grew as quiet as a graveyard. The only source of light originated from the back bedrooms of the house, filtering through the gaps in the shed's plank walls.

Pete tried the door more than once, causing the heavy chain to rattle. No luck there.

"Are we cooked?" Kathy asked.

"I doubt it," Tom answered. "They can't be stupid enough to hurt us."

"Sure they can," Pete argued. "They got themselves into this mess, didn't they? They're awfully dumb, I'd say."

"Well, they have to catch us first," Leslie said.

A mystified Kathy broke the stunned silence that followed. "*What* did you say?"

"Catch us?" Suzanne. "Whatever do you mean, Leslie? We're well and truly caught now."

"In fact, we're dead," Pete argued.

The older woman chortled. "This isn't just a shed. It doubles up."

Kathy asked, "What does that mean?"

"It's a storm shelter. When I was a child, we had tornadoes out here. My father built the shed for storage, but he dug an underground shelter first."

Tom was incredulous. "You mean—there's a storm shelter beneath us?"

"Yes, with room enough for all. No way will they find us. There's a trapdoor—right here." She thumped the wooden floor.

"No kidding?" Pete asked, hope rising in his voice. "Where does it lift?" His hands rifled through a thick layer of dirt and dust.

"I'll show you," Leslie said. "It's too heavy for me." She grabbed a hand—Pete's—and drew it over to the center of the shed. She pushed aside someone's leg. "There's a thin metal rim outlining a square. Got it? On one side, you'll find a narrow gap three fingers wide like a crack in the floorboards. Slip your fingers *under* it—it's a handgrip, almost impossible to see, even in broad daylight. Give it a good yank."

"Got it!" Pete said, his voice ringing. He tugged, but the trapdoor wouldn't move. "It won't budge."

"What did you expect?" Leslie bugged. "It hasn't moved in sixty years. Someone give him a hand."

Tom knelt on the floor and followed Pete's lead. Together the boys each slipped the fingers of one hand into the crevice and counted down, "Three—two—one... *Pull!*" The trapdoor lifted with an odd grinding sound.

A collective soft "Hooray!" rang out.

"All of you stand up," Pete ordered. "Backs to the wall." There was a shuffling of feet.

"Okay. Everyone out of the way?" he asked. Murmurs rippled around the shed. The boys lowered the heavy trapdoor backward, allowing it to land with a soft thud.

In the darkness, Tom reached tentatively down into empty space. "Hey, there are stairs going down."

"My father didn't expect us to jump. Follow me." Leslie pushed herself over to the cellar opening and lowered herself down to a solid wooden step. She started down. "Eight steps to the bottom. Who's next?"

Two minutes later, everyone but Pete was standing in the storm cellar.

Pete, still halfway down the steps, said, "Okay, so I close the trapdoor behind me, right?"

"That would be the idea," his sister quipped.

Whoomph!

16

NOISES IN THE DARK

"Lock it!" Leslie ordered.

"The trapdoor?" Pete said.

"What else are we talking about? There's a big sliding bolt. Push it to your left."

Pete felt around with his fingertips. "Got it." He slid the bolt into place and stepped down into the pitch blackness in which they were now immersed.

"Now what?" Suzanne asked.

"No matter what, we're in trouble," Kathy announced.

"Duh!" her brother said.

"Now we search for matches," Leslie replied, ignoring their comments.

"Down here?" Tom asked.

"Yes, down here," Leslie snapped. "And a kerosene lamp too, I hope."

Moments slipped by before Leslie's hand touched a box full of old-fashioned wooden matches. "Right where I remember them." She dug one out and struck it on the side of the box. Three matches failed to ignite before the fourth one flared up, its flame piercing the darkness.

"Hooray!"

The filthy glass chimney of a kerosene lamp diffused the flame. Soon, it glowed up, revealing the storm cellar in all its glory—bare earth floor and walls, an earthen ledge on one side, three wooden chairs half rotted away, an enameled steel commode, and four plastic water jugs.

"Dry," Kathy noted. It comforted her to see everyone's face in the surreal light.

"What, no food?" Pete asked.

"You'd want to eat sixty-year-old food?" Suzanne asked.

"What about oxygen?" Tom asked. "How long can we breathe down here?"

"My father thought of that," Leslie said. "There's a hidden metal pipe in here leading to the roof of the shed."

"Dad thought of everything," Pete retorted.

"You're being awfully rude," his sister said, poking him.

"Impertinent, I would say," Leslie said, glaring at him. Her nostrils flared. "Do that again, and I'll throw you out."

Suzanne asked, "What now?"

"We wait them out," Tom replied. "What else can we do?"

"I agree," Leslie said. "They'll leave soon enough. As stupid as he is, even Marsden must realize it's the end of the road for his sleazy little scheme—whatever it is."

Each one found a spot on the dirt floor. Thirty minutes dragged by before Suzanne wondered out loud, "How late is it?"

"Around ten, I'd guess," her brother replied.

Not much later, talking in a hushed tone, Kathy was in the middle of her favorite ghost story. "Then a floating white robe appeared and—"

The chain rattled on the shed's door, a muted but unmistakable sound.

"Shh!"

They sat frozen, not moving a muscle, listening, before the chain thudded to the ground. Then, silence. Seconds passed.

"That's odd," Leslie whispered. "Someone unlocked the shed and pulled the chain free. But the door didn't open."

"You're right," Tom agreed. "We would have heard those hinges squealing. Give it another minute before one of us scouts around."

"It could be a trap," Suzanne warned.

"Yeah. Or maybe someone's trying to help us," Tom said. "Otherwise, why bother? It makes little sense."

"Me," Pete said. "I volunteer to go up."

"Wait a sec," Kathy said. "I'm coming too."

"No you're not."

"Try and stop me."

Pete counted out the last few seconds to himself. "Okay," he said, stepping onto the stairs. "I'm on my way."

Kathy was right behind him.

Pete slid the bolt free and pushed the trapdoor up, lowering it as softly as he could despite its weight and the awkward angle. The siblings crept to the shed door and pushed. It opened. They allowed themselves just enough room to squeeze out, which minimized the squealing.

The Brunellis tiptoed over to the house's bedroom windows and peeked in. A man lugged a computer table down the hallway.

"They're still loading," Pete said, his voice low. "This is our chance—could be our only one."

They ducked and raced back into the shed.

"*Get out!*" Kathy hissed, leaning over the storm cellar. She held her hand out. "Quick."

Leslie stepped up, followed by the twins. Hurrying outside, Tom's sharp eyes searched the ground for his cell phone. No luck, but he found Suzanne's.

"They're still here," Pete whispered in a hoarse voice. "We've got a chance—over the ridgeline and down the hillside. Ready?"

Leslie hesitated. "I'm not sure I am."

"It's down, not up," Pete said.

"No fooling," she replied, obviously annoyed.

"Leslie," Tom said, taking her arm, "don't worry. If you get out of breath, we'll carry you. Let's go. It's our only shot."

One by one—nervous, silent, and bent low—they hurried to the ridgeline and traipsed downward. The two girls led the way, followed by Leslie. The boys were last.

Tom touched the emergency number for his father on Suzanne's phone. The Chief answered on the second ring. The story tumbled out in a breathless rush.

"Where are you now?" the Chief asked, his voice clipped. Tom heard a car door slam and pictured his father jumping into his unmarked police sedan.

"We're heading down the hillside."

"Okay, good. Get out of there. Help is on the way." They disconnected.

Halfway down, a blood-curdling scream stopped them in their tracks.

"*What was that?*" Kathy gasped.

"Who, not what," her brother retorted.

"It came from the top of the ridge," Leslie said. "Whoever it was just paid a price."

"What do you mean?" Suzanne asked.

"Someone saved us," the older woman replied. "My guess is that Marsden figured out who." She grinned. "He's not a happy camper."

"Whoa, I think you might be right," Tom conceded.

"That was a woman's scream," Pete said.

"Uh-oh," Kathy said, panicked. "We've got company!"

Sure enough, bouncing headlights revealed a car heading over the ridgeline and down the hillside road.

"We'll never make it to the bottom," Pete blurted out. "Let's peel off into the hillside."

They spun away from the roadway. The twins lined up on either side of Leslie, reaching for her arms.

"Cut it out," she protested. "I'm no invalid."

Suzanne cried, "They're stopping. Hit the ground!"

All five flattened themselves into foot-high wild grass. There was shouting. A car door slammed.

Bam! Bam!

"Shooters," Leslie whispered. "Oh, my Lord."

"They're not aiming at us," Suzanne hissed. "The shots are coming from the other side of the car."

"Must be that fox they mentioned on our first walk," Kathy quipped.

The wail of a siren pierced the night.

"Two sirens," Suzanne noted as the sound grew closer. "And a third."

The reaction on the hillside road was instantaneous. Doors slammed before the car pulled a U-turn and raced back up to the ridgeline. Other cars started up, and tires crunched on gravel.

Tom shouted, "Hey, they're escaping via the north road!"

"Who cares?" Kathy exclaimed. She jumped to her feet, arms raised straight into the air. "They're leaving. We win!"

17

A HERO EMERGES

Tom called the Chief again. "Dad, the bad guys are taking the north road away from the ranch house."

"Okay, got it. I'm on my way."

"They're still armed."

"I figured."

"A woman screamed on the ridge. We're turning back to help her."

The Chief hesitated. "You sure they've all left?"

"Almost positive."

"Okay, be careful. I'll be there in ten minutes."

A quick hillside conference took place. "Whoever that woman is, she needs help," Tom said. "But someone has to walk Leslie down."

She balked. "I'm fine; you don't have to worry about me."

"Not worried," Suzanne said, smiling. "But I'll walk you down." She felt responsible for the older woman. After all, it was Suzanne who had answered the door when Leslie appeared, seeking their help—less than a week before. One of Kathy's jokes popped into her mind: *But for a quirk of fate, she'd show up in your family tree.*

"Okay," Tom said, agreeing with his sister. He glanced at the Brunellis. "Let's go."

Suzanne and Leslie continued down toward the cemetery. The other three sprinted back and soon crested the ridgeline. They paused, catching their breath and checking for danger. Every light in the ranch house blazed. Leslie's Caddy sat in the parking area alone—the other vehicles had all disappeared.

They ran over to the garage, lit up inside bright as daylight.

"Whoa, what a mess," Kathy said. Crushed cardboard shipping boxes and shredded paper and other garbage littered almost every square foot of the floor.

They crossed into the house and searched room by room. There was evidence of a hasty departure—newspapers, paper, food trays, empty water bottles, junk of all kinds spread everywhere—but no sign of a woman.

Kathy found a flashlight on the kitchen counter coated with blood. She held it gingerly, with two fingers, and passed it to her brother.

"*My* blood," Pete said with a wry smile, touching his head. It still hurt. "We can use this though."

"There's not a soul anywhere," Kathy said. "Maybe they took the woman with them."

"Let's search the grounds," Tom suggested.

They walked out through the garage, crossed the gravel parking area, and circled the ranch house. The flashlight beam blazed a path. Nothing. Looking over the ridgeline below, they could see that Cemetery Hill had become a parking lot. Blue flashing lights were spinning atop several police cars, their sirens now muted. A television truck had arrived. Two vehicles were on the way up the hillside road.

"The shed," Kathy said. "It's the only place left." They ran over.

"They chained the door!" Pete exclaimed.

"Anyone in there?" Kathy shouted. She knocked, hard. Silence.

They raced back to the house and scrounged around before finding a hammer. Pete soon attacked the lock, whacking it again and again—*bang, bang*—until it fell to the ground in pieces. Tom grabbed the chain and yanked it free. Kathy ripped the door open.

Pete aimed the flashlight's beam into the interior. "Empty."

Kathy said, "Okay. Now I'm worried."

"Wait a minute," Tom said, looking at the floor. "When we escaped, we left the trapdoor open, right?"

"Yes!" Kathy shouted. They bent down and yanked on the trapdoor's handhold. The door lifted, easily this time, and crashed backward. Pete shone the flashlight into the storm cellar.

"Harriet!" Kathy screamed. The young woman lay across the dirt floor, her head tilted at an awkward angle, her long, flowing red hair spread asunder. Blood soaked the ground beneath her.

The three rushed into the shelter. Pete felt for her pulse. "It's irregular." Kathy cradled Harriet's head in her lap, trying to avoid the blood.

Tom pulled out Suzanne's cell phone and touched his father's emergency number.

The Chief answered on the first ring. "We're in the parking lot. Where are you?"

"Out back, in the shed. We found the lady from Cemetery Hill, the receptionist. She's hurt and unconscious. We need paramedics fast!"

"Got it."

Seconds later the Chief and Detective Ryan were looking down into the storm cellar. Heidi Hoover was right behind them.

"Paramedics are on the way," the Chief said. "How bad is she?"

"She got hammered on the head," Kathy replied. "There's serious bleeding and her pulse is irregular."

"Who is she? What happened?" the detective asked.

Kathy said, "Her first name is Harriet, and she works in the Cemetery Hill reception center. She's the one who picked Philip Marsden up from Emma Brown's boarding house to take him to—well, somewhere."

Pete said, "Which turned out to be a ruse."

"But we don't know her last name," said Tom.

Detective Ryan said, "We'll get that, no problem."

"Marsden and Maxwell locked us in the shed," Tom explained. "They had no clue about the secret storm cellar."

"The ranch was Leslie's home when she was a kid," Pete said.

"Someone freed us," Kathy added. "We think it was Harriet who removed the chain and walked away. We were halfway down the hillside when we heard her scream."

"Okay," Detective Ryan said. "So this woman saved you, and Marsden and Maxwell figured it out. She paid a serious price for being a hero. Pete, that's a nasty cut on your head. Did they do that too?"

Heidi took notes. "A hero, huh? People love that."

Paramedics arrived. They lifted Harriet out of the cellar and onto a gurney—a photographer from *The Daily Pilot* captured the moment. An ambulance rushed her to Prescott Regional Hospital.

Meanwhile, an evidence team descended upon the ranch house. Suzanne and Leslie followed them up in the twins' car. This time, as Leslie said, "Driving in style in this nice Chevy."

Leslie greeted the officers with, "I told you, didn't I?" But she was civil to them, bordering on friendly. The Chief and Detective Ryan admitted she had been right, forcing a smile to Leslie's face.

With the help of several police flashlights, the mystery searchers located their missing cell phones. Leslie had left hers in her purse, tucked away on the floor of her Caddy. "I'll call Pat," she said. But her purse had disappeared—money, wallet, credit cards, cell phone —everything but her keys that still hung in the ignition.

"Can you *believe* it?" she said. "That little maggot will be the death of me yet."

"Here, take mine," Suzanne said, handing her cell phone to Leslie. The older woman grumbled and thumped the hood of her car. Only then did she call Pat.

The four friends quizzed Detective Ryan.

"Any sign of them on the north road?"

"Nope. We didn't reach the intersection in time."

Pete asked, "Well, if they returned to Prescott, you'd catch them, right?"

"On Willow Creek Road? Sure, we've got it blocked off. But they won't do that—they know we're looking for them. There are multiple ways to access the city."

"What's the next move?" Tom asked.

"Thanks to those license plate numbers you provided, we can easily locate the two contractors. We'll question them tonight."

"What about Marsden and Maxwell?" Suzanne asked.

"Nothing yet," Detective Ryan replied. "We have an APB out for their arrest. Any ideas on where they'd hide out?"

The foursome shrugged but Leslie piped up. "What about checking with that lying rat at the funeral home? What's his name?"

"Aaron DeMaso," Kathy replied.

"Yeah, him," Leslie said darkly. "He lied through his teeth. He told you"—she locked eyes with Detective Ryan—"that Philip Marsden had passed away. And he handled the funeral arrangements, right? Dead, my foot! Though he will be, if I ever get my hands around his neck!"

Secret smiles were held back.

The boys returned the green groundskeepers vests, hanging them on the barn door. Then the foursome stopped at the hillside gate to retrieve the technology club's camera and motion detector.

It would be a long while before they ever returned to Cemetery Hill.

"The longer, the better," Kathy quipped.

18

THE SCHEME REVEALED

The next morning—Saturday, only a week after Leslie's unannounced visit to the Jacksons' home, but what a week!—Kathy called early.

"What now?" she asked. "Pete thinks we should visit Harriet at the hospital."

"I agree," Suzanne said. She placed the call on speaker at the breakfast table. "We need to thank her. Without Harriet, we'd have spent the night in that dreary cellar."

"Or worse," Tom said. "Those two guys are mean."

Suzanne messaged Detective Ryan. *OK to visit Harriet?*

Yes, he replied. *Her last name is DeMaso. Then stop in at the station.*

The Brunellis picked up the twins. Kathy drove as the foursome discussed the detective's message.

"DeMaso? Like Aaron DeMaso?" Kathy asked. "Is it possible—?"

"That they're married?" Pete replied. "Sure, that explains a lot."

"Yeah, but would those guys hurt Aaron's DeMaso's *wife?*" Suzanne wondered out loud. She looked out the window. "Maybe they are that ruthless."

The Brunellis' mother, Maria, greeted the four in Emergency.

"Harriet has a broken arm and a few gashes with lots of stitches. You'll find her recovering in Surgical Services, three-fifteen."

An elevator delivered them to the third floor. They found the darkened room down the hall, to the left. Suzanne stopped at the door, peeked in, and called out Harriet's name quietly. Harriet turned and looked at them. Her eyes widened in recognition.

"Thank God you're okay," Harriet said, her voice subdued.

They walked into a narrow room and approached her bed, two on each side. Harriet lay at a slight angle, her right arm in a sling, her head bandaged. Someone had shaved her flowing red hair a little on one side.

"Harriet, was it you who unlocked the door of the shed?" Kathy asked, taking her hand. "Was it you who freed us?"

"Yes." Harriet's voice cracked. She looked away. "They were talking about—hurting you. I—I couldn't let that happen."

Suzanne said, "When you say 'hurting' us…"

"Too horrible to talk about," Harriet replied.

"And that's why they threw you into the cellar?" Tom asked.

"When they realized you had escaped, they beat me," she replied, turning back to face them. "Then they tossed me down into that secret room. None of us knew of it, but you left the trapdoor open when you escaped. Philip went crazy. After that, I remember nothing."

"How did they figure it was you?"

"I was the one who objected to their horrible plans."

"What about your husband?"

"My husband?" A quizzical look crossed her face. "I'm not—oh, you mean my *brother*, Aaron."

"Your brother!"

"Yes. Aaron attended college with Philip Marsden and Robert Maxwell. That's where they met. Those two guys are evil." A tear rolled down her cheek.

"So Aaron wasn't there last night?" Tom asked.

"No, he was working with a family, planning a large funeral. And he'd never have consented to their evil plans."

93

"What were they doing at the ranch?" Suzanne asked. "We never figured it out." The four hung on Harriet's every word.

"They were running an online Ponzi scheme," Harriet replied.

"What's that?" Kathy asked.

Tom lit up. He had studied them. "It's a scam, a kind of fraud, in which the criminal promises investors a big return on their money, but instead of investing it, he only pays them with money from new investors—and on and on. Meantime, he siphons cash off for his own purposes."

"Oh, yeah," Pete said. "And he needs a constant flow of new suckers to keep the money rolling in. Kind of like a pyramid scheme."

Harriet nodded her head. "Yes. Philip convinced Aaron they were all going to get rich, so Aaron provided the initial seed money. Marsden is a genius with computers. Maxwell too. The money flow had just begun, but then you showed. Right away I knew it was over. I hated the whole idea from the beginning. I mean, pretending Philip was dead—how long could that work?"

She blew her nose. "And then Marsden's picture appeared in *The Daily Pilot*. That threw him into a spiral of rage. Crazy."

She scanned their faces. "Thank goodness you got involved. Old Blue Dog Company targeted retirees online—lower-income people desperate to make money on their meager savings."

Harriet sobbed. "It was horrible. He'd clean out those poor folks, leaving them with nothing. And he couldn't care less."

The foursome exchanged looks. It was obvious that they had tired the young woman out.

"We'd better go," Suzanne said soothingly. "We'll come back tomorrow."

"Please do," she replied. "I'd like to see you again. I have no friends left. Even my brother won't return my calls."

"Any idea where Aaron is? Or Marsden and Maxwell?" Pete asked.

"No, I wish I did. I'm worried about my brother."

"Thank you, Harriet," Kathy said. "You'd didn't have to rescue us.

We're very grateful." There was a murmur of agreement. The two girls each gave her a hug.

"You're a hero," Tom said.

"No, I'm not."

"Yes, you are, Harriet," Suzanne said. "And we'll speak up for you with a loud voice." That brought on another stream of tears.

The four jumped into the Chevy and headed for police headquarters. They soon met up with the Chief and Detective Ryan and took over one of the larger conference rooms.

"We interviewed Harriet earlier this morning," the detective said. "So we heard her story. What did she tell you?"

"Lots," Kathy said. "It was a giant Ponzi scheme."

"Yup, and a good one," the detective said. "If it wasn't for y'all, it might have worked."

"Harriet realized the plot would fail the day we showed up at the cemetery's reception center," Pete said.

"The scheme was working, just the way Philip had imagined it," Kathy said. "Harriet says Marsden is a technical genius. The money was pouring in."

The Chief chuckled. "That's true, but it turns out he's not as smart as he thinks."

"That's a fact," Detective Ryan said.

"We asked where her brother might be," Suzanne said, "but she didn't have a clue."

"We do," the Chief said. He set a cup of coffee on the conference table in front of him. "Mr. DeMaso turned himself in this morning. He appeared here with his attorney."

"Whoa," Suzanne said. "Harriet will be glad to hear that. Did he talk?"

"He sure did," Detective Ryan said, nodding his head. "The man was very contrite. And he's furious that Marsden and Maxwell hurt his sister. Guess what else bugs him? Forging a death certificate. Aaron says he failed to live up to the code of honor of his profession by doing that. The document is routine, and he knew that no one would question it. And you'll never guess which 'private hospice' our friend Philip checked himself into: DeMaso Family Retreat—which just happens to have the same address as DeMaso Funeral Home.

"So," Kathy interrupted, "that explains why Aaron made up that story about Marsden dying at Prescott Regional Hospital."

"Exactly," the investigator replied. "He had to turn your inquiries regarding Philip Marsden's death as far away from DeMaso Family Retreat as possible. But to be fair, Aaron cooperated and answered every one of our questions—except one."

"The hideout of the two ringleaders?" Pete guessed.

"Right. He doesn't know where they are, and we don't, either," the Chief replied. "Not yet, anyway."

"Marsden and Maxwell have gone to ground," Ryan added. "We arrested the two other programmers this morning, but they were just paid help. Well paid, I might add. Enough to keep their mouths shut while the operation was going. We'll charge them too."

The Chief took another sip of coffee. "Thanks to the pics you captured, we're looking for a late-model Nissan sedan registered to Robert Maxwell in Tucson. We checked out his address, but the man moved three months ago."

"That makes sense," Kathy said. "By then they were planning the Ponzi scheme. So he moved to Prescott."

"We believe he rented a place," the detective said. "Under a phony name, I'd guess. Wherever that is, there's a good chance they're holed up there."

The Chief said, "The scheme blew up in their faces. They'll skip town when things die down."

Detective Ryan grinned. "They don't have most of their hardware. The coders drove off with it. But unfortunately they *do* have the source code."

"Uh-oh," Suzanne said. "That means they could start up again tomorrow. That's not good."

"What about tracing their cell phones by cell tower triangulation—or even GPS reporting?" Tom asked. As a technology guy, Tom knew cell tower triangulation could locate cell phones to within about three-quarters of a mile, and GPS sometimes with near pinpoint accuracy.

"We tried," the detective replied. He raised his hands, palms up. "The programmers shared those cell numbers with us. But for either of those methods to work, a cell phone has to be *on* and receiving a wireless signal." He shrugged. "Technical guys like these are smart—Marsden and Maxwell have gone dark."

Suzanne sat straight up. "Hold it. They stole Leslie's purse. I'll bet *her* phone is on!"

19

BUSTED

Detective Joe Ryan fed Leslie's cell phone number to an operator. An hour later, a uniformed officer walked into the conference room holding a slip of paper.

"Here's the address you're looking for, sir. We were lucky."

The investigator adjusted his new glasses and looked down. Then he passed it to the Chief. "It's a private residence, not a mile from here. I'll bet it has a garage, and they've hidden that Nissan in it."

"Okay, excellent work," the Chief said, his face beaming. "Leslie left her mobile phone on. Great idea, Suzie. Congratulations!"

She held back a big grin, but the other three rallied around her. Even her brother gave her a rare hug.

Detective Ryan was on his cell phone, setting up a raid. Police cars would converge on the house from four directions.

"Come on," the Chief said, inviting the group to join him. "Let's watch the fruits of your labors." Twenty minutes later, they parked a few doors away from the suspected hideaway. All eyes were on the residence while they waited with bated breath.

Soon, four different police cars converged on the house. Detective Ryan stepped out from his vehicle, bullhorn in hand.

"Philip Marsden and Robert Maxwell." Ryan's voice boomed through the neighborhood. *"Prescott City Police have surrounded you. Step out with your hands up."*

One officer held a barking German shepherd on a leash. There was nowhere to go, no place to hide.

The detective repeated his exhortation before the two men slowly walked out the front door. They surrendered, hands in the air, eyes downcast. Neither spoke a word.

Minutes later, the foursome found Leslie's purse, lying on the floor in the back of the late-model Nissan—hidden in the garage, just as the Chief had expected. The cash and credit cards had disappeared, but the criminals hadn't noticed her cell phone, stashed in an inner pocket—with a Missed Call notification on its home screen.

It was over. An elaborate, lucrative, and worldwide online Ponzi scheme had failed.

———

ON SUNDAY MORNING, *THE DAILY PILOT* LANDED ON THE JACKSONS' driveway with a soft thud. Tom raced out to get it.

"Wow! Suzie, you gotta see this," he yelled upstairs. "We made the front page!" He spread the newspaper across the kitchen table as his parents scrambled out of the way. Suzanne rushed down.

Their mother chided the twins while the Chief chuckled to himself. "It's exciting, but it's not *that* exciting."

The story on page one blazed out "Dead man walking" and displayed the Florence State Prison photo of Philip Marsden.

"Heidi got her headline," Tom said, glancing at his sister with a grin.

A subhead read, "Online Ponzi scheme broken." The dramatic story unfolded, complete with a shot of Harriet being wheeled into an ambulance. Her caption read, "A hero emerges."

A third photo showed a group shot of the four looking into the lens—with Leslie standing in the exact center. "Prescott natives save retirees from fraud," read the caption.

One paragraph mentioned the mystery searchers—"By name!" said Suzanne, feeling quite proud—and their cooperation with Prescott City Police. "Without citizen involvement,'" Tom read aloud. "'Detective Ryan stated that the Ponzi scheme ring could have run under the radar for years. We also owe a debt of gratitude to Mrs. Leslie McPherson of McPherson Construction, Detective Ryan noted.'"

"That's a nice photo," Sherri said, pointing to the picture. "Leslie looks good too."

"Great job," the Chief noted. "And nice coverage for her business."

"We're sure proud of you," their mother added, looking at the twins.

"Thanks!" Tom said.

"I'm grinning like a fool," Suzanne grumbled. "What an awful shot."

"What's to complain about?" her brother asked. "Looks just like you."

"When I want your advice, hotshot, I'll—" Her cell phone rang. She raced upstairs. It was Kathy.

"Did you see *The Daily Pilot*? What a great photo!"

Suzanne groaned.

20

A GUEST OF HONOR

A week passed before the families gathered together for a special Italian dinner at the Brunellis'.

Harriet—the guest of honor—sat in the family living room, one arm in a sling. She had arranged her beautiful red hair in such a way that it hid the shaved area on her head, with its still-healing staples The dinner was a big thank-you to Harriet for rescuing the four young mystery searchers.

"The thing I don't understand," Leslie said, "is why they robbed my cash box. I mean, with all that money coming in, who needs a lousy five grand?"

"I can answer that, Leslie," Detective Ryan said. He set a glass of mineral water down on a side table. "The funds rolled into a Swiss bank account by electronic deposit. But the bank required signed hard copies—notarized too—of a wire transfer agreement for withdrawals before they would free up the cash. That's why that envelope showed up in the overnight UPS delivery."

"Talk about luck," Pete said. "We just happened to be there when the driver dropped it off."

"Good thing you spotted it," Suzanne said, her eyes darting to Tom.

"That's right," Harriet said, picking up the story. "They ran out of Aaron's seed money and needed more to pay the two programmers. But my brother refused to put in another dime. It was a desperate situation—if the coders walked, everything would come to a screeching halt. Then, out of the blue, Marsden said he knew where he could lay his hands on enough cash to carry them through for a few more days."

"That's when he cleaned you out of your five grand," the Chief said, looking at Leslie.

"Fifty-two hundred," she said before muttering something unintelligible. A shocked look crossed Pat's face before she shushed Leslie.

That exchange sent Heidi into a conniption of laughter before she spoke up for the first time. "I have a question too. Why did Philip Marsden steal Old Blue Dog Company? Why didn't he just form a new corporation?"

"Oh, that's easy," the Chief said. "Foreign banks are more likely to view new corporations with suspicion because of money laundering. The Swiss bank would check out Old Blue Dog Company as a routine matter. And guess what? The company officers—Zeke and Leslie McPherson—were clean. No criminal or civil actions against them, and no complaints against the two-year-old company. It was a slam dunk."

Detective Ryan picked up the story. "Marsden couldn't use his own name in case of a criminal background check. So he switched out Zeke as a corporate officer... and Maxwell became the new president."

"So Old Blue Dog Company was a gift that dropped into Marden's lap," Joe said. For the Brunellis' father, the jigsaw puzzle all came together.

"Did it ever," Tom said.

Something puzzled Maria. "Marsden faked his own death. So who's in his gravesite on Cemetery Hill?"

"Not who, what," Harriet replied sheepishly. "Aaron dropped a hundred-pound bag of salt into a cheap casket." People smiled at the revelation. In an odd way, it was a relief.

A few minutes later, Leslie floored the twins' parents. "You know, we all came close to being related." Her hands twirled in the air as her eyes flashed around the room.

The Chief, taken by surprise, chuckled politely. "You're right, Leslie. My father dated you in high school."

"You knew about that?"

"Sure. Dad told me years ago. You were popular."

She looked at him. "Yup, pretty too. I flipped a coin. Your dad lost—Zeke won. He was the lucky one." She was serious too.

The foursome glanced at one another—and at the bemused expression on the Chief's face—trying desperately not to laugh. None of them had ever met anyone quite like Leslie McPherson. Nor did they expect to.

Kathy hurried to change the subject. "Detective Ryan, how much time will Marsden and Maxwell serve in prison?"

"No way of knowing," he replied. "Their court appearance isn't for another month. But Marsden violated the terms of his parole—we won't see him again for many years. And remember, they're both being charged with a lengthy list of offenses: fraud, theft, false imprisonment, assault with a deadly weapon, and attempted murder. I wouldn't want to be in their shoes."

Out of respect for Harriet, no one brought up Aaron's name. But it hung there, crossing everyone's mind.

Sherri sat beside Harriet. Over the past few days, they had become fast friends. As a county social worker, Sherri had helped the traumatized young woman navigate the problems she faced in her life. Every so often Harriet teared up, including now.

"It's difficult when they arrest a family member, but this too will pass," Sherri said to comfort her. "Aaron is a decent guy, and he's never been in trouble with the law before. Plus he has cooperated with the police. I expect his sentence will be lenient."

"That's true," Suzanne added. "And his sister is a hero. That can't hurt."

"I'm not much of a hero," Harriet protested.

"Well, we're here to disagree," Kathy said. The foursome gathered around Harriet and gave her a collective high-five.

"Dinner is served," Maria announced. "Antipasto salad and chicken marsala. And for desert my family favorite, tiramisu. Harriet, you're first."

Everyone cheered, but the twins were beside themselves. *"Mmm-mmm."*

LATER, JUST AS THE LUSCIOUS DESSERT APPEARED, SUZANNE RECEIVED a text message. She felt her phone vibrate in her pocket. Who would message her now? Her immediate family and closest friends were all gathered around the Brunellis' dining room table.

Suzanne excused herself and stepped out into the hall. The text was from Mrs. Otto, a neighbor for many years, and the manager of Prescott's St. Vincent de Paul thrift store. It read: *Hi, Suzie—Just received a raft of old books from an estate. Might be something you'd like among them. See u soon.*

Suzanne couldn't wait.

EXCERPT FROM BOOK 5
THE TREASURE OF SKULL VALLEY

Chapter 1
The Swamp

"What is it?" Kathy Brunelli yelled as she gazed up, shading her eyes from the blazing Arizona sun. "What do you see?"

Her brother, Pete, stood high on the adjacent bluff, right beside his buddy Tom. He cupped his hands and shouted back down to Kathy, his voice echoing off the surrounding cliffs. *"Wilderness! . . . -ness! . . . -ness! . . ."*

"Brilliant," Kathy groused to her best friend, Suzanne Jackson, Tom's twin sister. "Sometimes Pete can annoy me without even trying."

The two boys stepped back from the edge of the bluff and disappeared.

The treasure map showed water, and close by too. But where? Suzanne glanced at the compass in her hand. "What are those guys *thinking*? If we follow the map, it's as obvious as the nose on your face—look where it ends." The girls eyed the document for the umpteenth time.

Kathy said, "Well, that big 'X' centers on water, that's for sure. Or at least, there was water when someone drew this map—but who knows how long ago *that* was."

The unknown "someone" had sketched the map in black ink across the top half of an 8x11 folded sheet of writing paper. He—or she—had traced a journey from Prescott to Skull Valley, a twenty-mile jaunt through Arizona's spectacular high country. Then the trail jogged onto what had turned out to be a little-used gravel road, which split into two.

That's when things got interesting.

The adventure had begun two days earlier with a text message from Mrs. Otto: *Hi, Suzie—Just received a raft of old books from an estate. See u soon.*

Mrs. Otto was the Jacksons' longtime friend and neighbor, and the manager of Prescott's St. Vincent de Paul Thrift Store. When it came to handling books, Mrs. Otto trusted Suzanne implicitly, and not just because Suzanne was such a book lover: she was also a confident young person, reliable and sure of herself, someone who knew where she was going in life. Yes, Mrs. Otto had seen Suzanne's famous temper flare, more than once too, but over the years she had watched as Suzanne slowly gained control of her fiery emotions.

The donation had appeared on the charity's loading dock at an unknown time during the night—dozens of tomes, all boxed up, in good condition or better. Old ones too. Ten boxes in total.

The anonymous gift bore a cryptic message, attached to one box with heavy packing tape: *The lady died.*

Suzanne hurried over on Monday morning. Her job—a part-time gig she loved—was to sort and price each book. An hour later, as she flipped through an early copy of *Wuthering Heights*, a folded sheet of paper slipped out and fluttered to the floor. Suzanne's heart skipped a beat—it wasn't the first time she had discovered treasure between the pages of a book.

There had been the forgotten tintype of a Confederate war officer. In perfect condition too—the thrift store sold it for seventy-five dollars. Once she had found an eighty-year-old birth certificate. And, just last winter, a hundred-dollar bill had popped out of a famous historical novel. It looked pristine but dated back to the 1920s. *Wow.*

After that, Suzanne fanned every book. But finding a treasure map raised the ante to a whole new level.

"Oh, my goodness," Mrs. Otto said when Suzanne laid the find on her desk. Her eyes grew larger as she adjusted her glasses and tilted her head a touch. "I'm sure this is someone's idea of a joke. Still, you might check it out, dear. One never knows."

It was the title above the sketch—"My Treasure Map"—that fired up everyone's imagination. And beneath the drawing, written in cursive with a shaky hand, someone had penned a curious set of instructions:

Take Iron Springs Road (county road 10) to Skull Valley. Turn left on Copper Basin Road, 6.3 miles. Turn right to switch to the secondary road, go 1.3 miles. Park, and walk left along the dry creek road for half a mile. Watch for the water! Please help, whoever you are. Thank you.

"Skull Valley? Treasure? *Man, oh, man,*" Pete had said when Suzanne showed the treasure map to the twins' best friends. He rubbed his hands together. Pete was the impetuous one who acted first, thought second, and often paid a price for his impulsiveness. "Can you *believe* it?"

Tuesday morning found the foursome walking along an old, wide track that ran parallel to a dry creek bed, twisting its way north. A century earlier, someone—miners, no doubt—had turned the route into a rough roadbed. But time had dredged up rocks and boulders, layering them against dead trees and broken, decaying branches, littering the track for as far as they could see. At one point, decades earlier, a gigantic desert saguaro had fallen along the route and rotted away to its skeletal remains.

The map's initial instructions—Iron Springs Road to Skull Valley, turn left on Copper Basin Road to a secondary road—had turned out, despite the passage of time, to have been easy enough to follow. But not even a 4x4 could have been able to negotiate the debris on the old miners' track, never mind the Brunellis' low-slung Mustang Hatchback.

Kathy parked at the side of the secondary road, ready to hike in. But first the boys climbed that bluff, searching the arid land before them.

"Notice anything?" Tom asked.

"Nothing but an incredible view," Pete replied.

In the distance stretched the million-plus acres of Prescott National Forest, rising from low desert to mountain ranges over eight thousand feet high, and home to Grief Hill, Yellowjacket Gulch Blind Indian Creek, and Horsethief Basin. Looking east, between where the boys stood on the rocky bluff and the western edge of the national wonder—lay an undulating and barren high-desert landscape: rock-strewn ravines, hidden canyons, sparse hills, cactus and trees.

"You can count on wild mule deer down there for sure," Tom said knowingly, "plus antelopes, cougars, bears." It was by no means their first desert hike.

"And snakes," Pete added with a wicked grin. "Western diamond-back rattlers. Kathy's favorite."

The boys raced down the far side of the bluff and crossed back over a canyon floor. Panting and out of breath, and despite being weighed down by their backpacks—with rope, flashlights, compasses, an axe, a hammer, bear spray, and, most importantly, food—they soon caught up with the girls, who by this time were well ahead of them along the trail.

Tom admitted defeat. "Okay, you were right, Suzie. We couldn't spot a drop of water anywhere."

"*Told* you," she replied with a touch of exasperation. "The treasure map will find it for us. And we're close—according to the map, it's dead ahead. Let's keep going."

The desert floor felt frozen in time: utterly still, without a hint of a breeze. The foursome's footsteps and labored breathing joined a million cicadas and the screeching alarms of overhead birds. A relentless sun beat down on them, intensifying as the minutes dragged by and midday approached, but they had dressed for it: shorts, cool tops, hiking boots, and hats.

Pete stopped for a giant swig of water from his canteen. "Might be the only liquid out here."

Suzanne rolled her eyes. "Get ready for a surprise." As the discoverer of the map, she felt the most invested in believing in its accuracy. In her mind, there wasn't a shred of doubt.

Soon, Kathy's pedometer clicked to point five. "We're close—watch yourselves."

The old mining track inclined a few degrees as it meandered between low canyon walls. Then it sloped up to a plateau with a gentle eastward turn before slipping downward into a ravine, and—

"*Water!*" Kathy cried.

They all raced forward. A large, irregularly shaped pond stretched before them, looking as if it had swallowed the roadbed. The water's surface—coated with a slimy layer of decayed moss and other green matter—displayed tall, reed-like stalks poking above it, stretching from murky depths up into the air. A pungent smell of dead greenery assailed their nostrils.

"You call that water?" Tom quipped. "More like a swamp, I'd say."

"Boy, you're not kidding," Pete said. "So the old mining route heads straight into a slimy pool of—well, whatever this is. Then it climbs out of the ravine and continues north."

"Yeah, a hundred yards farther out," Suzanne said, sounding more surprised than disappointed. She had anticipated water, but not this stagnant desert oasis.

"No wonder we couldn't spot it from the bluff," Tom said, taking in the soaring canyon walls. "You realize how *deep* this ravine is?"

"It's deep all right," Kathy said. "We're in a natural bowl, surrounded on all four sides. The only open channel is this track, coming and going."

"Check out the chalky white deposits on the rock walls," Suzanne said. "Calcium, I bet. The water has receded since spring."

"So the treasure's . . . here?" Kathy said. She held the map in both hands in front of her.

"It sure looks that way," Pete replied, peering over her shoulder and jabbing the X. "And that's where we are. Whoever drew this map knew the area well."

Kathy knelt and slipped a finger into the water, pushing aside a thin layer of slime. "I'll tell you what," she said. "No way am I jumping into *that* to look for anything."

"You big baby," Pete teased with a grin. "Me, I'll go in there. But first I need food to fortify me."

"I'm with you, buddy," Tom said, clapping his best friend on the back. "Eating, I mean." Laughter rang out.

Soon, a blanket lay stretched over a flat slab of rock beside the murky pond. Each one of the hungry four found a spot to relax. They unpacked sandwiches and snacks and passed bottles of water around.

"I wonder what's hiding in there," Suzanne wondered aloud.

"You don't think there are snakes under the slime, do you?" Kathy asked in all seriousness. She wrinkled her nose.

A thought popped into Tom's head. "No clue, but you can bet this must be the watering hole for the local wildlife."

"That's why I packed bear spray," Pete said. "You can't ever know what you'll encounter out in the wilderness. Not only that, but it's possible the treasure's in a nearby cave."

That threw his sister into a conniption of laughter. "Oh, yeah. And that imaginary cave might hide a fat, hungry black bear, right?"

"Wouldn't be the first time."

"We'll follow you in," Kathy added.

"Kind of you, I'm sure."

"Whoa, that never crossed my mind," Suzanne interrupted, looping back to her brother's comment. She cast her nervous eyes around the ravine, searching for signs of wildlife. "Slime or no slime, this is the only water for miles. We need to head out long before sunset."

"Yeah," Pete said grinning, "before that bear gets thirsty."

His sister gave him a good poke in the side.

Their discussion next centered on how to explore the pond. Tom suggested building a raft and measuring the depth with a sheared-off tree branch.

"No way," Suzanne countered. "Too time consuming."

Pete liked the branch idea. "We can plunge it in there and see what we're dealing with. Any sandwiches left?"

Minutes later, as Kathy peered across the swamp, she caught a glint in the afternoon sun. *What is that?* she wondered. Without saying a word, she stood and walked to where the miner's track vanished beneath the water. She paced along the water's edge, varying her angle of vision, before dropping to one knee.

Suzanne munched on an apple. "What's up, Kathy?" she called out between bites. "What are you looking at?"

"Oh, I'm just checking out this vehicle sunk in the swamp," she replied innocently, eyeing her brother.

"Vehicle!" the other three chorused.

Pete stood up. "What on earth are you talking about?"

Kathy giggled and pointed ahead, toward the pond's dead center. She loved one-upping her brother. "Check it out. What's sticking out of the water, a foot high, between all those stalks?"

The three hurried over. Silence descended as they peered across the murky surface, following Kathy's pointing finger. A thin sliver of metal protruded above the layer of slime, almost hidden by a forest of reeds. It had a tiny nodule on top, and its peeling chrome was pocked with rusty brown patches. Not twenty yards from where they stood.

Tom broke the silence. "It's an antenna!"

"Oh, sure, I see it," Suzanne said. "The old-fashioned kind."

"Like the one on our antique Mustang," Pete said.

"Uh-huh, no kidding," Kathy said, poking her brother once more. "And I'd bet anything the treasure is inside this one."

Hi, fellow mystery searchers!
I hope you enjoyed this sneak peek at
The Treasure of Skull Valley

Pick up a copy at your favorite retailer today!

And be sure to sign up for special deals
and to hear about new book releases before anyone else.
You can register here:

https://www.mysterysearchers.com/the-series/

BIOGRAPHY

Barry Forbes began his writing career in 1980, eventually scripting and producing hundreds of film and video corporate presentations, winning a handful of industry awards along the way. At the same time, he served as an editorial writer for Tribune Newspapers and wrote his first two books, both non-fiction.

In 1997, he founded and served as CEO for Sales Simplicity Software, a market leader which was sold two decades later.

What next? "I always loved mystery stories and one of my favorite places to visit was Prescott, Arizona. It's situated in rugged central Arizona with tremendous locales for mysteries." In 2017, Barry merged his interest in mystery and his skills in writing, adding in a large dollop of technology. The Mystery Searchers Family Book Series was born.

Barry's wife, Linda, passed in 2019 and the series is dedicated to her. "Linda proofed the initial drafts of each book and acted as my chief advisor." The couple had been married for 49 years and had two children. A number of their fifteen grandchildren provided feedback on each book.

Contact Barry: barry@mysterysearchers.com

ALSO BY BARRY FORBES

Book 1: The Mystery on Apache Canyon Drive

A small child wanders across a busy Arizona highway! In a hair-raising rescue, sixteen-year old twins Tom and Suzanne Jackson save the little girl from almost certain death. Soon, the brother and sister team up with best friends Kathy and Pete Brunelli on a perilous search for the child's past. The mystery deepens as one becomes two, forcing the deployment of secretive technology tools along Apache Canyon Drive. The danger level ramps up with the action, and the "mystery searchers" are born.

Book 2: The Ghost in the County Courthouse

A mysterious "ghost" bypasses the security system of Yavapai Courthouse Museum and makes off with four of the museum's most precious Native American relics. The mystery searchers, at the invitation of curator Dr. William Wasson, jump into the case and deploy a range of technology tools to discover the ghost's secrets. If the ghost strikes again, the museum's very future is in doubt. A dangerous game of cat and mouse ensues.

Book 3: The Secrets of the Mysterious Mansion

Heidi Hoover, a good friend and newspaper reporter for *The Daily Pilot*, introduces the mystery searchers to a mysterious mansion in the forest—at midnight! The mansion is under siege from unknown "hunters." *Who are they? What are they searching for?* Good, old-fashioned detective work and a couple of technology tools ultimately reveal the truth. A desperate race ensues, but time is running out.

Book 4: The House on Cemetery Hill

There's a dead man walking and it's up to the mystery searchers to figure out "why." That's the challenge from Mrs. Leslie McPherson, a successful but eccentric Prescott businesswoman. The mystery searchers team up with their favorite detective and utilize technology to spy on high-tech criminals at Cemetery Hill. It's a perilous game with heart-stopping moments.

Book 5: The Treasure of Skull Valley

Suzanne discovers a map hidden in the pages of a classic old book at the thrift store. It's titled "My Treasure Map" and leads past Skull Valley, twenty miles west of Prescott and into the high desert country—to an unexpected, shocking and elusive treasure. "Please help," the note begs. The mystery searchers utilize the power and reach of the Internet to trace the movement of people and events. . . half a century earlier.

Book 6: The Vanishing in Deception Gap

A text message to Kathy sets off a race into the unknown. "There are pirates operating out here and they're dangerous. I can't prove it, but I need your help.' Who sent the message? Out where? Pirates! How weird is that? The mystery searchers dive in, but it might be too late. *The man has vanished into thin air.*

Book 7: The Heist Forgotten by Time

Coming – Fall/Winter, 2020

Don't forget to check out
www.MysterySearchers.com

Register to receive *free* parent/reader study guides for each book in the series—valuable teaching and learning tools for middle-grade students and their parents.

You'll also find a wealth of information on the website: stills and video scenes of Prescott, reviews, press releases, awards, and more. Plus, I'll update you on new book releases and other news.